"You're not a reporter, are you?"

Hannah laughed nervously, unable to lie to this man's face. "Of course I am. Breaking in to strangers' houses on major holidays is how I work."

"I see." Jack half smiled, and she realized with more guilt and a twinge of satisfaction that he thought she was joking. Advantage Hannah. Except then he started looking her leisurely up and down, at her short, clingy sequined dress, and she didn't feel as if she had the advantage anymore. At all. "You didn't come here with...other ideas?"

"*What?* Why would I do that? I didn't even know you were going to be home." Oops.

His eyebrows went up. "Where did you think I'd be?"

"Uh, I got lost in the storm. I told you."

"Yes, you did." He held her gaze, and she controlled her hot and flustered self enough to look back steadily.

Except the second she relaxed her guard, she started thinking about how much she wanted Jack to kiss her and how sexy and romantic it would be right here in this dim hallway. He could back her up against the wall and have his multibillion-dollar way with her.

Mmm...

Blaze

Dear Reader,

Who wouldn't want to be trapped in a sumptuous mansion for twenty-four hours with a sexy gazillionaire? Raise your hand. Nobody? No one? Not surprised. What if you found out then that he wasn't who he claimed to be?

I love books where people aren't quite who they seem. It's not only a great source of conflict between characters, but it's a great fantasy, to think we have an inner self vastly different from the one we project to the world. Closet geek? Vixen? Kinky freak? Childlike goofball? A terrifying and thrilling part of falling in love is discovering the secrets of your lover and then revealing yours.

In twenty-four hours Hannah and Jack manage to create a raging storm between them equal to the one outside. Put on your mittens and enjoy! And have a wonderful and exciting 2009 filled with your own fantasy romance come true.

Cheers,

Isabel Sharpe

www.IsabelSharpe.com

Isabel Sharpe

NO HOLDING BACK

TORONTO • NEW YORK • LONDON
AMSTERDAM • PARIS • SYDNEY • HAMBURG
STOCKHOLM • ATHENS • TOKYO • MILAN • MADRID
PRAGUE • WARSAW • BUDAPEST • AUCKLAND

Recycling programs
for this product may
not exist in your area.

ISBN-13: 978-0-373-79448-5
ISBN-10:   0-373-79448-7

NO HOLDING BACK

www.eHarlequin.com

Printed in U.S.A.

ABOUT THE AUTHOR

Isabel Sharpe was not born pen in hand like so many of her fellow writers. After she quit work in 1994 to stay home with her first-born son and nearly went out of her mind, she started writing. After more than twenty novels for Harlequin—along with another son—Isabel is more than happy with her choice these days. She loves hearing from readers. Write to her at www.IsabelSharpe.com.

Books by Isabel Sharpe

Don't miss any of our special offers. Write to us at the following address for information on our newest releases.

Harlequin Reader Service
U.S.: 3010 Walden Ave., P.O. Box 1325, Buffalo, NY 14269
Canadian: P.O. Box 609, Fort Erie, Ont. L2A 5X3

To Lori H,
for being there every day to whine to

1

"SO THERE I WAS IN PARIS at one of the greatest restaurants in the world, and stomach flu picks *that night* to turn on me, between the *pigeon aux olives* and the *baba au rhum.*"

"Oh, no. Imagine that." Hannah O'Reilly swallowed another mouthful of tepid champagne and glanced desperately behind the large pallid lump named Frank who'd inflicted himself on this portion of her evening. At a New Year's Eve party in an ostentatious mansion outside of her home city of Philadelphia, wearing one of those dresses saved all year for parties like this, she should be dancing wildly with a hot stranger. If she wanted boredom, she could have stayed home.

A waiter wafted by with a tray of tidbits. Hannah grabbed one, not sure what was in it, but assuming it cost more than her daily food allowance. Gerard Banks, owner of both this house and the newspaper that employed her, *The Philadelphia Sentinel,* threw a fancy New Year's Eve party every year for his staff, friends and family. Hannah didn't know which category this guy Frank belonged in, staff, friend or family, but she wished he'd bludgeon someone else with his stories. She was here for a healthy serving of hedonism.

"Another time, in London, I ate an oyster and felt movement between my teeth." He mimicked checking in his large mouth and pretended to hold something up. "Turned out to be a worm. Never ate oysters after that."

"I don't blame you." She laid her hand on his jacket sleeve to cushion the rejection. "You know…I think I'd like a refill on my champagne. It was great talking to you."

"Sure." He sighed and lifted his soda in a resigned toast. "Happy New Year."

"Same to you, Frank." She escaped, breathing a guilty sigh of relief, maneuvered between a chatting couple and a chartreuse settee, set her glass on a table full of similar empties next to the stone hearth and went searching for a champagne-bearing waiter. Then she was going to find some wild single hottie and flirt her head off. Because she was determined that this new year would launch a fabulous new chapter of her life. Careerwise, familywise and manwise. Out of the rut, into the rutting.

Bingo. Tuxedoed waiter ten paces ahead, carrying a tray of fizzing delight. She dodged between a ficus and a ceramic statue of a leopard. With any luck she could cut him off on the other side of the orange suede couch, and—

"Hannah, how's the year winding down for you?" Tragically, her boss, Lester Wanefield, neither wild nor single nor with an extra glass of champagne, stepped into the few remaining feet between her and her next dose of bubbly. "Hey, now don't *you* do good things for red sequins."

"Oh. Thanks." She loved how she looked in this dress, but enticing her boss made her wish she'd worn sackcloth.

"Great party, huh?"

"Mmm, yeah." If she could keep herself from thinking the money should be used for something more worthy. Like charity or education or disease research or Hannah's bank account.

She kept her eye on the waiter. This could still work. If he moved a few feet to his right and glanced her way…

"I've been thinking about your next assignment. Not for your Lowbrow column, but a feature story. Maybe start it on the front page."

Lester had her full attention then—all rotund, gray-bearded, bespectacled, five-foot-six-inches of him. Now that she'd been at the paper over a year, she'd been pestering him—well, hinting first, suggesting second, pestering third—for more substantial assignments than the powder-puff stories he'd been tossing at her and burying in the back sections. "That would be fabulous, Lester. You know, I've actually been researching a story. There's a little-known side effect of the drug Penz—"

"A story about boobs."

If she punched him in his large stomach, would he squeal like the pig he was? "Boobs."

"Women who've had boob jobs, to be precise. How does having a bigger rack alter their dating habits, their sex lives, their ability to attract men and does it change the type of men they score with?"

"How…interesting." He had to be kidding. "But I was actually hoping to do—"

"We'll call it 'Rack of Glam.' And I want lots of pictures." He leered at a well-endowed woman strutting past. "*Lots* of pictures."

"I'd rather—"

"I know you would, O'Reilly. But you don't get your 'rathers' in this business until you've been around a lot longer than you have."

"So you've said." *Ad nauseam.* "But I—"

"No butts." He gave her bare shoulder a condescending squeeze and winked. "Just boobs."

Ew.

She approximated a smile, knowing further argument would only cement his opposition. But grrrrrr. How much girly news could a nongirly woman stand? Girly dress tonight aside.

She needed to find a story on her own, something bigger

and sexier than the drug side effects, something so compelling that even Pig Lester couldn't turn it down. A huge scoop with enough popular appeal to hook him, but enough substance to further her career and get her on such sound financial footing that if her parents' lives imploded again she could be the one they could depend on.

Like…

Like…

Yeah. Like that.

She blew out a breath and spotted another waiter, wished her boss a Happy New Year that she barely managed to keep from sounding like *Damn You and Your Family to Hell,* and followed, determined to score more alcohol, this time to numb the frustration. A story about boobs. Whoopee. The year ended in approximately fifteen minutes and as far as she was concerned, good riddance. Landing what she thought would be her dream job hadn't worked out. Again. Her last boyfriend hadn't worked out. Again. Her determination to lose ten pounds hadn't worked out. Again. Twenty-nine years old and she thought she'd be set for life by thirty.

At least circumstances had miraculously turned around for Mom and Dad. Though fat lot of help she'd been able to be.

The waiter stopped to serve an evening-gowned trio. This was her chance.

"Hannah." Her closest work-friend, business reporter Daphne Baldwin, snagged her hand and dragged her into the library. "You have to meet this person…Dee-Dee something. Royco or Rosmer or Rrrrrr…I forget. But you have to meet her."

"Why?" Hannah glanced wistfully at the top of the retreating waiter's head, his tantalizing tray just visible above the crush of people. So close, and yet…

"Because, she's…wait." Daphne searched the room and frowned. "She was just here."

"Where's Paul?"

Daphne made a face. "He wouldn't come. Said he didn't see why he should get dressed up in uncomfortable clothes and hang around people he didn't know and didn't want to know, when he could stay home and be comfortable drinking without having to worry about driving drunk."

He had a point, though Hannah wouldn't dare admit it out loud. There were times she felt Daphne's mellower half would be happier with a woman who matched his nonenergy, and that Daphne needed more of a live wire, but Daphne insisted he was her life's ballast. Hannah thought he was more her life's punching bag. "So you're a wild single tonight. He better watch out."

"I don't know, Hannah, he's been acting weird lately. Doesn't want to do anything with me."

"You mean he no longer jumps to do everything *you* want to do?"

"Ha ha ha." Daphne continued to scan the crowd, unperturbed by Hannah's bull's-eye zinger. "I'm serious. He's been distant and…I don't know, unresponsive. Like there's something really bugging him, but he won't tell me."

"Do you think he's cheating?"

"What?" Daphne's horror was immediate, and so impressive that nearby heads turned.

Oops. Where was the Reverse button on this conversation? Obviously Hannah had struck a nerve, and it wasn't her place to torture her friend by planting suspicions. "No, no, I don't think he is, I just… Isn't that what you always suspect when—"

"Paul would never cheat. He doesn't have the time. Or the initiative."

Oof. As much as Hannah loved Daphne, sometimes she thought Paul *should* cheat, just to stop her from taking him for granted. "Something at work?"

"He'd tell me that. It's probably a midlife crisis. Men get those all the time, don't they? Serves them right for not being slaves to hormones every month like we are." She frowned and plunked her hands onto her enviably trim hips. "Now where the heck is that woman?"

"Why do I need to meet this person?" Hannah sighed, queasy over her friend's relationship attitudes and feeling generally cranky. She didn't want to make small talk with any strangers, not even Mr. Hot-Wild-Single-Whoever. The dress was wasted. The night was wasted. The year was wasted. Her life was on its way to being wasted. Only *she* wasn't wasted because the damn waiters were avoiding her.

Fine. She'd ring in the New Year, butt-kiss Gerard for spending gazillions on people he underpaid, and get home to the city before the predicted ice storm hit. Too bad about her fantasy of spending the night enraptured with a new love, but probably just as well. It was always the same tired story. She fell for men like stemware during an earthquake, then when they sensed the depth of her passion and excitement and hope for the future, they abruptly moved on. No matter how hard she tried to act indifferent, men could always tell. Maybe she should make a resolution tonight to avoid the gender altogether.

"Come on." Daphne dragged her out of the library into another room, some sort of study, then another huge garish living room, as if the front living area the size of Hannah's entire apartment wasn't enough. "Don't see her here, either. Let's go back."

"Ooh, wait." Hannah caught a glimpse of Rory, the VP of advertising whom she had a minicrush on, standing alone, looking a little lost. At the office Rory barely acknowledged her in her usual attire of jeans and baggy sweaters. Should she test her slinky red-sequined minidress out on him and see if he—

Argh! What was she, some kind of addict? Ten seconds and

she'd already forgotten her resolution. *Men bad, Hannah. Alone good. Alone safe.*

Alone, boring and predictable.

"Let's try this way."

Hannah dug in her feet before Daphne could continue bull-dozing. "Would you mind telling me what is so thrilling about this person?"

"Oh. Right. Duh." Daphne thwacked her forehead, making her fabulous brown curls bounce. "She's close to Jack Brattle."

Zip. Hannah's gaze left Rory's tall form at light speed and fixed on her friend. "*Jack Brattle?*"

"Knew that'd get your attention."

"Where is she?" Hannah grabbed Daphne's rock-muscled arm, not even indulging her usual envy for Daphne's discipline in the gym. "Find her. An interview with Jack Brattle could get me—"

"I know, I know, world renown and riches galore. Why do you think I wanted you to meet her?" Daphne pulled Hannah—or was Hannah now pulling Daphne?—toward the house's huge foyer into which spilled a staircase worthy of Scarlett O'Hara's Tara. And at this staircase, oh happy day, Daphne proceeded to point. "There she is."

And there she was, a little-black-dress-clad platinum-blond bombshell cliché, sauntering down the steps on requisite spike heels. A perfect candidate for Lester's "Rack of Glam" article.

"I'm sorry, is there a Pamela Anderson look-alike contest tonight?"

"Shh." Daphne positioned herself at the bottom of the staircase. "Hi, Dee-Dee."

"Hey." Dee-Dee reached them, shook back her mane of peroxide and flicked a glance at Hannah. "Cool dress."

"Thanks. Thank you." Hannah gave her best ingratiating grin. "I love yours, too."

"This is Hannah O'Reilly. She works with me at the *Sentinel*."

"Yeah?" Another shake of overcooked hair.

"She writes the Lowbrow column."

"Oh!" Something approaching life quivered in her too-taut face. "I love your column! You're always fighting with that guy who writes the Highbrow column, D. G. Jackson. Too funny!"

"Yes!" Hannah gritted her teeth. Way too funny. Mr. Jackson took malicious delight in thumbing his nose at her column, which extolled the virtues of inexpensive food and entertainment around the city of brotherly love, while his dwelt on places and things no normal person could afford and no sane person would waste that much money on. She'd responded to one particularly degrading remark by sending him a case of Grey Poupon and blogging about it. He'd reciprocated with cans of spray-cheese. Word got out, and now both their editors were fanning the flames…all in the name of circulation and buzz.

Circulation and buzz. Yeah, superdeedooper. What about the news? She wanted to write news.

"So…what does this D.G. guy look like?" Dee-Dee tipped her head and started playing girlishly with a fried strand, making Hannah want to tell her D.G. could be Liberace's surviving twin. "His articles are so charming and funny and classy all at the same time."

"I've actually never met him." Hannah smiled, aching to change the subject to Jack Brattle—where was he, how soon could she meet him? "But maybe I can arrange to set you up sometime for lunch."

"Oooh, I'd love that. I have this feeling about him…" She giggled. "Would you really do that for me?"

"Sure, no problem." Hannah hadn't been serious, but it

didn't hurt to promise one favor right before she asked for another. And maybe she could work a date with the grievously tacky Dee-Dee into another joke on Mr. Highbrow. "So…Daphne tells me you're best buddies with Jack Brattle."

"Oh." Blink-blink of false eyelashes. "I don't know about best buddies. I shouldn't even have told—"

"Friends, though?"

"Well." She looked uneasily between Hannah and Daphne. "I've…met him."

Hannah sent Daphne a sidelong glance. *Met* was a far cry from *close to*. "When was this?"

"Oh, a while back." She gestured vaguely. "I'm really not supposed to tell. It just sort of slipped out."

And thank God for that. Jack Brattle had kept himself out of the public eye as effectively as his late gazillionaire father had kept himself in it, which meant the absence of a Brattle in the news left that much bigger a hole.

An interview with Harold Brattle's son and heir… Or, given that Dee-Dee was full of hot air as well as silicone, even snippets of inside information on Jack's whereabouts, his habits, tastes, sexual preference… Any reporter would give up major organs for that scoop.

Many had tried, none had succeeded. Not since the disappearance of Howard Hughes had a missing person generated this much mystery and excitement. Yet by all accounts Jack Brattle continued to run his father's empire while remaining invisible. From time to time people claimed to have encountered him—like people kept seeing Elvis—but the sightings always turned out to be hoaxes or misidentification.

"Whatever you can tell me would be great. I'll handle it all very discreetly. No one will ever be able to trace anything back to you."

"Oh gosh. I'm *so* not supposed to."

"I know." She laid a sympathetic hand on Dee-Dee's soft arm, wanting to pinch her. "I completely understand. I've put you in a really tough position."

"Well…" Dee-Dee bit her bee-stung lip. "I do know where he lives. A guy I met once took me by his house. I guess it wouldn't hurt to tell you that."

"Really?" Hannah's droopy spirits perked up. Rumors had been flying that Jack owned property in the area, but his cover had been scrupulously complete. Or at least he hadn't walked down any local streets with a giant name tag on. "You are amazing, wow."

"In West Chester." Apparently now that Dee-Dee had started, the confession had gotten easier. "My friend said he's abroad until spring, but the house is not that far from here."

Hannah's reporter lust started rising. Around them the chatter intensified as enormous flat-screen TVs in several rooms flickered on, and crowds gathered to watch midnight approach.

"Can you tell me how to get there?"

"Well…yeah. I could. But he's away. And I'm really not supposed to."

"Simple curiosity on my part. I wouldn't try to go in or bother anyone. Just drive past. No one would ever know I'd been by." She smiled her most innocent smile, shrugging as if it didn't matter all that much if Dee-Dee spilled or not. *Please. Please. Please.*

"Well…okay. You got paper or anything?"

"I have a BlackBerry." She nearly gasped out her relief, fishing the life-organizing electronic device out of her adorable dress-matching red-sequined bag as fast as she could before Dee-Dee changed what there was of her mind. "So what does he look like?"

"Oh, he's…" Dee-Dee gestured expansively and raised her eyes to the ceiling. "You know."

"Ah. Yes." Hannah's heart sank even as she opened a new memo, ready to write down directions. Dee-Dee definitely hadn't met him. Probably didn't even know which house was his. This would turn out to be another attention-grabbing hoax. She better prepare herself for the disappointment right now. And yet, on the crazy minuscule chance this could be legit… "So where does he live?"

She poised her fingers over the tiny keyboard and waited. Several minutes later, she'd written down Dee-Dee's directions, which consisted mostly of phrases like "turn left at that big stone thing" and "stay on the road even when it looks like you shouldn't."

A miracle if she found it. And an even bigger one if there was anything to find.

Excitement swelled in the room. Someone started a countdown from sixty seconds. Hannah slipped the BlackBerry back into her evening bag, then snagged—*finally*—a second glass of the slightly sour champagne from a passing waiter and turned to face the screen, counting along with everyone else.

As soon as midnight came and went she'd find Gerard, thank him for a wonderful evening and set out on her hunt for the wild and elusive Jack Brattle, heir to his father's real estate fortune which could, of course, given that Dee-Dee didn't seem qualified for Mensa, be nothing but a wild-goose chase.

She lifted her glass as the shouting started. *Five, four, three, two, one…*

Or…she could scoop every other reporter in the country and make this a really phenomenal start to the rest of her life.

2

HANNAH PRESSED HER FOOT gingerly on the accelerator, peering through the windshield into a curtain of sleet, bouncing *tzap-tzap* off the glass and tinkling on the roof of her beloved bright red Mazda, which she'd named Matilda. Hannah considered herself a very persistent investigator, but even she was questioning how smart it was to be out here so late in this mess with no one around. Pennsylvania's gentle rolling countryside surrounded her car. Despite the beauty of the fields, forests and sloping hills, she did not want to slide off the road and end up spending the night in any of them.

Amazingly, Dee-Dee's directions had held up so far, which fueled her determination to keep going. Hannah had found "the stone thing" and she even recognized the "amazing tree." The woman might not radiate brainpower, but, whether or not Hannah found the Jack Brattle pot of gold at the end of this rainbow, Dee-Dee obviously had a sharp eye and a killer memory. All Hannah had to do now was turn down a driveway where the gates were "kind of creepy and jail-like." Not to mention, "not very visible from the road unless you were looking."

She was looking; she just wasn't seeing.

The sleet fell harder. A driveway crept by; Hannah peered toward it. No gates.

"Come on, Jack's house." At this point, she just wanted to

see the damn thing, mark the address so her BlackBerry could find it again, and come back when the weather wasn't intent on killing her. Of course hindsight was now sitting on her shoulder whispering that she would have done a lot better to come back later in the first place.

Next driveway. No gates. Phooey. Properties weren't exactly close together out here in Billionaireland. Everyone needed his own private stable, pool, tennis court, golf course…all the basic necessities of survival.

Her BlackBerry rang. She dragged it from her bag, which she'd flung onto the passenger's seat, and glanced at the screen. Dad, calling to wish her Happy New Year. If she didn't answer, he'd worry. She eased Matilda over to the side of the road and turned on her flashers.

"Happy New Year, Dad."

"Happy New Year to you, sweetheart." His rough slow voice crackled over the tenuous connection. "Why don't I hear party noise, you didn't go? Or do fancy parties not make noise?"

"I left after midnight. Wanted to get home before the weather turned bad."

"Is it bad now? I haven't looked outside in a while."

"Uuh, no. Not bad yet." The tinkles of ice crystals on her roof turned to sharp taps. In the white beam of her headlights pea-sized balls bounced and rolled on the asphalt. Hail to the chief. "The roads are fine."

"Okay. But call me when you get home. The storm is supposed to come on fierce."

Tell me about it. "I'm…seconds away, Dad. In fact, turning on my street now. How's Mom?"

"Better, still better. Always better, thank God. I don't know what we would have done without Susie."

"She's a blessing, for sure."

"Mom even fed herself part of her dinner tonight. I made lasagna."

"Good for her! Her favorite. That's wonderful." She smiled, ashamed of herself for not being grateful enough as the clock ticked toward midnight for the few good events of the past year. Dad's latest employer, The Broadway Symphony, on the brink of collapse, had been saved by a generous donor who wiped out the orchestra's debt and allowed her father to keep the first job he'd ever held down this long—going on five years now. And Susie, a nursing angel of mercy, had showed up at their door, highly recommended by Mom's doctor, offering to help out with Mom's rehabilitation right there in their home for practically slave wages, saying she needed the experience.

Before those miracles, Hannah had gone through agonizing feelings of helplessness with her own bank account in no shape to help. Prey to addiction and poverty, her parents hadn't done much to give her a secure childhood, but especially now that they'd climbed out of the pit, she wanted them to have a secure retirement. "Tell Mom I love her and that I know this year will have her back to her old self. I'll call tomorrow."

"I'll tell her. I hope it's a good year for you, too, Hannah-Banana." He coughed to clear his throat—a legacy of lifelong smoking. "Maybe a nice young man will come along."

"Maybe." She rolled her eyes. Yeah, maybe. Maybe he'd even stick around longer than a few weeks or a month. And maybe cancer would start curing itself and global warming spontaneously reverse.

"You take care of yourself. Drive safely."

"I will. Love you, Dad." She ended the call with another pang of guilt as the sleet continued to bombard Matilda, collecting on the roads at an alarming rate. This was crazy. If anything happened to her, what would it do to her poor father who'd already had his relatively new sobriety and stability threatened with her way-too-young mom's shocking stroke and his livelihood nearly yanked out from under him?

Hannah was being selfish. She should turn around now and crawl home, give up this crazy quest until the weather was better.

Except she'd already come this far… And it was *Jack Brattle*. What if someone else in the business had overheard Dee-Dee? What if Hannah lost this huge long shot at a scoop? What if? What if? What if?

She put Matilda in gear and moved slowly forward, wheels crunching ice. A flash of lightning made her jump and hold on to a wince while waiting for the expected thunder. Thundersnow. Whee. This only added to the fun.

Next driveway… No gates.

The wind started whipping in earnest, sending Matilda into a shimmy. Hannah narrowly avoided a largish branch on the road. Snow mixed with the sleet to reduce visibility further.

Oh goody.

Next driveway. She had to turn in and focus her headlights to see…

Gates! Creepy dark jail-like ones! Eureka. She'd found it. Or found something.

Out came her trusty BlackBerry. She called up the GPS system and noted her location. Bingo. Adrenaline rushed out to party. She had Jack Brattle's address. 523 Hilltop Lane, West Chester, Pennsylvania.

Tomorrow she'd come back to—

More lightning. Close. A mere beat later thunder cracked the sky over her car. Wind gusted.

Hannah went rigid in her seat. The gate had opened a crack, then swung back. She swore it had. Matilda inched forward, Hannah peering through the torrential snow-sleet.

There. There it went again. Unlocked? It certainly looked that way. And, according to Dee-Dee, who seemed to be on the up-and-up since her directions had panned out so far, Jack Brattle wasn't in residence. Hmm…

Wait, what was she thinking? He must have a full staff living on the estate and security up the wazoo. If she even crossed the property line she'd probably be surrounded by guard dogs and torn to shreds.

But maybe before they quite devoured her, she could get a glimpse of the house. After all, by now she had the perfect excuse. A lone disoriented traveler, lost on her way back from a party and… Help! Where was she? Could she depend on the kindness of strangers until the worst of the storm passed?

And by the way, while she waited, could she whip out her BlackBerry, take pictures of every room in the house and interview everyone old enough to speak?

They'd go for it. Sure they would.

Now. The gates. She fumbled under her seat for the umbrella she kept in the car. Of course it wasn't there. Where had she lost this one? Who knew?

No umbrella. And since she'd been to a party she was wearing her couple-times-a-year wool coat and not her everyday water-resistant parka with hood. Not to mention open-toed heels instead of warm fleece-lined boots.

Oof.

But okay, for Jack Brattle…

She dashed out of the car, whistling "This Could Be the Start of Something Big," one arm up to keep from being pelted, which accomplished pretty much nothing. But oh joy, it was worth every thwacking and stinging and drenching moment because, hot damn, the gate was really and truly unlocked!

Not only that, the hinges were beautifully oiled, so the

huge structure moved soundlessly and easily with one good shove. Was breaking and entering meant to be or what?

Back in the car, giggling with cold and nervous excitement and residual champagne, she applied her wet foot to Matilda's accelerator and then…

She, reporter Hannah O'Reilly, gained admittance to what she was starting to dare believe was Jack Brattle's estate, and got thwacked, stung and drenched pushing the gate nearly closed behind her.

Woohoo!

The long driveway curved through a wooded area thick with tall evergreens that blocked out the worst of the assault. A good thing because otherwise, given the current visibility, she could easily have ended up bumper to bark at some point.

Two or three tensely expectant minutes later—no attack dogs yet—the trees gave way to a large grassy lawn already frosted white. Matilda slid gracefully sideways on the last turn; Hannah reduced her speed, heart thumping even harder than it had been. She definitely did not want to get stuck here.

Another gust of wind rocked the car and sent snow flying nearly horizontal. Hannah pined briefly for her cozy—the politically correct term for *tiny*—apartment, for sitting safely in bed with her warming blanket heating the sheets, a good book in her hand, a hot mug of tea on her nightstand.

But then…no Jack Brattle scoop. After years of an unsatisfying career fund-raising while writing too-often rejected magazine articles and pieces for her neighborhood paper on the side, she'd managed to land a job in journalism, which she'd wanted since she was a kid and had written and produced her own paper: *Hannah's Daily News,* circulation, approximately four, including herself; number of issues: twenty. She still had them somewhere.

Another flash of lightning, a clap of thunder. The sleet rattled her roof in earnest now—could it really hail during a snow-storm?

She guided Matilda around the circular driveway, came to a stop opposite the grand front steps, complete with stone Grecian urns. Snow obscured the view, but it wasn't hard to tell the house was a colossal Colonial.

This wasn't how the other half lived, this was how the other millionth lived.

So…

Car in Park, she sat for a minute before switching off the engine. She really didn't want to drive all the way back to Philly in this mess. The roads were dangerous and the trip could take hours. Options were either to wait out the storm right here in Matilda…she had plenty of gas to run the heater periodically…or see if anyone was home. No lamps glowed in any windows, at least not in the front of the house, at least as far as she could see. The light shining over the entrance could be on a timer.

Nothing ventured…

She pulled the handle and nearly had her arm torn off as a gust of wind wrenched Matilda's door wide open. Her excitement gave way to jitters. This storm took itself quite seriously. Now she hoped someone *was* home, not only for the sake of her immortality-guaranteeing article, but to make sure she survived this.

Up the steps, she nearly slipped twice, squinting through the sting of ice, finally reaching the front door. Holding her breath, she rang the bell, then crossed her fingers for good measure and crossed her arms over her chest, strands of her ruined upsweep whipping her cheek, earrings turning into tiny daggers repeatedly flung at her neck. Another gust rocked her back on her probably ruined heels. Hannah made a grab at the house's front-door handle and miraculously stayed upright.

This was not that much fun. At least not yet.

Another poke at the bell, another shivery icy minute or so waiting, though by now she knew it was ludicrous. On New Year's Eve with the master abroad any remaining staff would have the night off, and if there were some type of butler or housekeeper on duty, he-she would have answered by now.

She stepped away and craned up at the facade to see if any lights had gone on in response to her ring. Though housekeeper-butler rooms would be in the back, wouldn't they? She wasn't that up on her mansion architecture.

A horrifically bright flash of lightning, a massive crack of thunder, a truly terrifying assault of wind. Hannah yelled and leapt toward the door, pressing herself against it for the tiny bit of shelter theoretically offered by the ledge above.

Then the odd impression of something dark swooping through the air in her peripheral vision, and the open-mouthed disbelief as the limb of a tree—large enough to be a tree itself—landed on her car.

Crash.

Hannah stared. Her mouth opened, but no sound came out. *Oh, Matilda.*

Her roof and hood were crumpled down to the seats, the windshield smashed. If Hannah had still been inside, she could be dead now.

Dear God. Delayed shock hit, funny breathing and all-over-body shaking that wasn't only from the cold this time. This was really, really not good. Really. When was she going to learn to curb her impulsive behavior? She knew this storm was coming. Jack Brattle's estate was not going to disappear overnight. Her parents and friends would say it again. *How many times do we have to tell you, look before you leap? Think before you act.*

Think, period.

Okay, okay. Staying calm. She had other more important things to worry about. Like not freezing to death.

Down the treacherous steps again, she tugged at poor sweet Matilda's door. It didn't budge. Slipping and sliding her way around to the other side, she pushed her arm through cold scratching branches to yank on the other door, even knowing the frame was too crunched to be able to open.

Oh Cheez Whiz. Her evening bag containing her Black-Berry was still in that car. Her GPS system would broadcast her location, but not until someone realized she was missing and tried to find her. Why had she told Dad she was already home safely?

Because he had enough to worry about.

She staggered back up the steps, huddled against the house's cold uncaring door again. Not for the first time she envied her mother and father their renewed commitment to each other after they got their lives back on track, their mutual caring and support. If she had someone now, the kind of man she dreamed about finding, he'd stop at nothing to bring her home safely.

Or he would have stopped her being such an idiot coming here tonight in the first place, and she'd be home safely in bed with him now, ringing in the New Year in one of her very favorite ways.

Tears came to her eyes and she blinked them away in disgust. Okay, game plan. She was responsible for herself and had been as far back as she could remember. Maybe there was a service entrance? Maybe someone in the house would hear her ring or knock from there? Maybe there was a cottage behind the house she could break into, or maybe her amazing luck would hold and there'd be a garage with the door left co-incidentally open…

Oh dear.

Another flash of lightning. Hannah turned away from it, burying her face in her hands, shoulders hunched, waiting for the smash of thunder.

Boom. More wind. Sleet pelting her back.

"*Stop.*" She grabbed the door handle and twisted desperately, knowing it would be locked and the gesture was completely—

The handle turned.

The door swung open.

She tumbled in, gasping with surprise, then relief, slammed the door behind her, closing out the terrible storm.

Did that really just happen?

Who the hell went abroad and left his front door open? More than that, what house of this size and value didn't have a dead bolt and a security system? She waited with held breath for the ear-splitting shriek of an alarm. *Whoop-whoop, intruder alert.*

Nothing.

Maybe he had a system that only sounded at the police station. One could only hope. Rescue would be welcome if the cops took long enough so she had plenty of time to look around. Because it was slowly dawning on her, now she'd escaped the possibility of hypothermia, that she could very well be *in Jack Brattle's house.*

Of course it was possible the door was open because someone had already broken in. Maybe some terribly dangerous criminal was right now prowling the floors above her.

She listened, listened some more, kept listening…and heard nothing, besides the distant hum of the heating system. Really, what kind of idiot would be out on a night like this?

Ha ha ha.

Maybe someone was asleep upstairs? Maybe he or she forgot to lock the gate and the front door after a particularly fun party?

"Hello?" She wandered closer to the staircase, barely visible from the light coming in through the front windows. "*Hello?*"

Nothing. She climbed halfway up, peering into the darkness of the second floor, and prepared to shout as loudly as she could. "*Anyone home?*"

Still nothing.

Most likely careless—or tipsy—staff or service people were responsible for the unlocked entrances. Maybe they'd intended to come right back and the storm had held them up or held them off. Whoever they were, she owed them a huge juicy kiss for inadvertently offering her shelter. Bless their ir-responsibility. She was not only going to survive the night, she was going to survive the night *inside Jack Brattle's house*—because she just had to say that again. *Inside Jack Brattle's house.*

That was assuming Dee-Dee was telling the truth, which Hannah would, because why would she go to all that trouble to send Hannah anywhere else?

Of course Mr. Brattle would have a phone so she could call for help right away, but…she didn't need it right away. Later would be fine. Far be it from her to make someone risk his or her life coming to rescue her now in this terrible weather. Right? Right.

Oh, this was a night for her memoirs. First, she needed out of these wet shoes and to hang her coat somewhere water-proof so drips from melting ice bits wouldn't stain the hardwood.

She fumbled at the wall near the door and struck pay dirt with a light switch that threw a soft chandelier-glow over the breath-taking entranceway. Hannah let her eyes feast in a slow circle around her. Parquet flooring, and thick vivid Oriental rugs that she lost no time in exploring with frozen toes after she kicked off her shoes and stripped off her sodden stockings. Mmm, bliss.

The house was warm—deliciously warm—so obviously whoever left was planning to come back soon. At least when he or she did, the storm, the open gates, open door and Hannah's devastatingly destroyed car provided the ideal justifiable excuse for her presence.

This could not possibly have been more perfect. Maybe being impulsive hadn't been so bad for once. Matilda—God rest her engine—would not have given her life in vain.

A promising set of louvered doors slid open to reveal, just as she'd hoped, a vast closet with an array of expensive coats—men's coats—in conservative shades of brown, black, gray and tan, suitable for the average heir. She brushed her hand over the textures—wool, cashmere, leather—sniffed the lingering hint of their owner's very nice cologne, then pushed past the wooden hangers for a metal one her damp coat wouldn't ruin. Down the hall to her left she discovered a first-floor bathroom in whose shower she hung her dripping woolen mess.

And now…to explore. *Jack Brattle's house.*

Kitchen first, glimpsed as she'd passed in search of the bathroom. *Ooh la la.* State of the art, but not detracting from the nineteenth-century feel of the entranceway. She skimmed her fingers over the built-in paneled refrigerator. Wouldn't she love to microwave a hot dog in a room like this? She bet it had never seen one.

Out of the kitchen, exploring room after room, not unlike Gerard Banks's house—and hey, how often did she score a two-mansion day?—but here there were no leopard statues, no large-screen TVs or—dare she say—gaudy furniture. Jack Brattle was all dark wood, leather, brick fireplaces, rich subdued colors in rugs, books, cushions. True old-money class.

She had to admit, in spite of her aversion to opulence, the house was incredible. The kind of place that brought to mind every fabulous manor she'd imagined while reading, from *The*

Secret Garden to *Jane Eyre.* And yet, a home she could imagine someone actually lived in, not redecorated every season to show off to visitors and lifestyle magazines.

Up the curving staircase to a landing with a comfortable-looking burgundy couch and gold patterned chair, another shelf of books and a window seat beside it. Down the hallway lined with portraits and landscapes, passing at least four bedrooms, a workout room, a study, another bedroom, apparently unoccupied like the others, and then, what she suspected was the master bedroom suite. Was this where Jack Brattle slept?

The glimmer of light under the door registered at the same time she pushed it open…

And came face-to-face with the wettest, handsomest naked man she'd ever been startled out of her wits to meet.

3

"OH! I'M SO SORRY!" HANNAH jammed her eyes shut and reared back into the dim hallway, slapping a hand over her closed lids for good measure. Oh, *no*. Oh my goodness, oh my...*goodness* what a sight. Even with her eyes closed she could still see—

No, stop. She could be arrested for breaking and entering, this was not the time to go lusty-wench. He could be calling the cops right now. *Reporter Busted for Ogling Billionaire's Bodacious Bod.*

"Sorry. I'm really sorry. I, um, got lost and your entrance was open and my car is—"

She sensed the door moving in front of her, slid two fingers apart and peeked through.

Gulp.

He was standing, towel wrapped around his, um, hips, ohhh, yeah, and, um, his chest was...whew. He... Wait. He was smirking. She apparently amused him. Or maybe he thought it was funny because he'd called a SWAT team, which was pulling into his driveway right now and unloading bazookas.

"I was, um...just saying that your door was open."

"You pushed it open."

"It was—" She realized just in time what he meant. "No. Downstairs. The front door. Was open. My car is outside with a tree on it. What I mean is, I got lost and the roads are bad and then, so I saw your gate open and then the car-crushing thing happened and I came in because you're unlocked in front, and I was freezing and thought the place was empty, so I started looking around, but…uh…but it's not, is it. Empty that is."

Silence. He looked even more amused, but as if he were trying hard not to be. God, he was gorgeous. Gor-gee-usss. If this was Jack Brattle, then he had to be emotionally bankrupt or deeply miserable because it was just not fair that anyone could have all that money and all that…everything *and* look the way he did.

"No, the house isn't empty. I'm here."

"Right. Right. I see that. I'm so sorry. I just needed shelter because I didn't…have any."

"Okay."

Are you Jack Brattle? She couldn't ask, because she wasn't supposed to know this was his house. But, of course, who else could be naked in the master bedroom? Stunningly naked, she might add.

"I'm Hannah."

"Jack."

Jack! *Jack!* It took every ounce of energy not to light up like a tree angel, blast off like a rocket, or fizz like a shaken Coke. Bless Dee-Dee and her gravity-defying boobs.

"Nice to meet you, Jack. I'm truly sorry to barge in on you like this. Especially—" She gestured to his towel without looking at it even though she really wanted to look at it, and at him. All of him. "—like this. My phone is in my car, which I can't get into. If I could use yours to call the—"

"Wait here."

She nodded demurely, then when he went back into his room and closed the door, she did a silent, hopping, fist-pumping victory dance in his hallway. Besides a front-page spread in Lester's "Rack of Glam" article, she owed Dee-Dee a hundred lunches with D. G. "Highbrow" Jackson for this. No, a thousand.

Hannah stopped dancing and put a hand to her hammering heart. Regroup. She was a pro. He was her subject. When he came back out, she needed to talk less—since she'd just broken the world record for disjointed babbling—and observe more. So far she'd observed that he wasn't very chatty, not that she'd given him much of a chance, and that he had no problem giving orders. "Wait here" was not the most charming way she'd ever been asked to linger. Though for all he knew she was a lying con-artist thief, so maybe a lapse in manners was forgivable.

She had also observed that he was the kind of male eye candy she liked best. Thick dark hair, none of this California surfer-dude stuff for her. A strong face, very masculine, stopping short of head-clubbing-caveman. Tall. Dark brown eyes that sent out a shock of attraction on contact, and that indicated copious brainpower behind them.

And—gravy on her stuffing—the man obviously worked out. Good shoulders, flat stomach and that great sculpted butt that—

"Sorry to keep you waiting."

"Oh. Well. That's okay." He'd put jeans over the great sculpted butt, which was disappointing because while she liked him naked just fine, she always thought of Jack Brattle in a tuxedo, kind of James Bondish. Were they thousand-dollar designer denim? Looked like Lees to her. "You certainly don't need to apologize. I'm the one who intruded on your—"

"I saw your car out my window. Impressive."

"I do things thoroughly."

"Uh-huh." He moved forward unexpectedly and took hold of her wrist—not very gently. "So what are you really here for?"

She gasped at his harsh tone, which took her completely

by surprise after his initial pleasantness. "To keep from freezing to death?"

"You're sure that's all?"

"Yes." In spite of her shock over his Jekyll-Hyde act, she felt a crazy pang of sympathy and a dose of guilt. Guys like Jack Brattle probably had people with ulterior motives surrounding them 24-7. Including her at the moment. "Why else would I be here?"

"You're not a reporter, are you?"

She laughed nervously, unable to lie to this man's face. "Of course I am. Breaking into strangers' houses on major holidays is how I work."

"I see." His lips half smiled, and she realized with more guilt and a twinge of satisfaction that he thought she was joking. Advantage Hannah. Except then he started looking her leisurely up and down in the short clingy sequined dress and she didn't feel like she had an advantage anymore. At all. "You didn't come here with…other ideas?"

"*What?* Why would I do that? I didn't even know you were going to be home." Oops. *Because I thought you'd be in Europe, Jack Brattle.* "I mean here."

His brow went up. "Where did you think I'd be?"

"I have no idea. I thought the house was empty, then I found out it wasn't. You left your door unlocked, so I—"

"You told me. I'm sorry if I insulted you. Women have— It's happened before, though not at this house."

"You have others?"

"Yes." He started looking her over again, and she got all flustered and a little heated up, when she really wanted to be annoyed and insulted. "And that *is* a very seductive dress."

"I was at a party."

"Where?"

"Malvern."

"You live in Philly?"

"Yes."

"Strange way of heading back to the city from there."

"I got lost, I told you."

"Yes, you did." He held her eyes and she controlled her hot and flustered self enough to look back fairly steadily.

Except the second she relaxed her guard, she started thinking about how much she wanted him to kiss her, and how sexy and romantic it would be right here in his twilit hallway. He could back her up against the wall and have his multi-billion-dollar way with her.

Mmm.

What would he do if she leaned forward right now and—

Stop it. Just stop. Had she learned nothing about herself and about men in the years since puberty? Not to mention she'd just become outraged when he suggested she was thinking exactly what she was thinking.

"Sorry about that." He relaxed his interrogation-stare, so apparently she'd passed the test. "I just have to be careful."

"Why?"

He winked. "Double-O-Seven stuff."

"Seriously?" She nearly swallowed her tongue. Had she not just been thinking James Bond? And here he was, the legend come to life, though she doubted he was actually doing anything but running his late father's business. A business, of course, she knew nothing about as far as he was concerned, so she'd play along. "You're a *spy?*"

"Not even close. What are we going to do with you?"

She had many ideas by now, none of which she could say out loud. But his abrupt change of subject away from the personal meant this could be a tough interview. "If you'll point me to a phone I can call Triple A and have my car towed."

Say no, say no, say no.

"Why don't you wait until this weather clears? I'm sure Triple A will have its hands full rescuing motorists who couldn't find conveniently unlocked, apparently deserted houses."

"If you're sure…" Stranded in a mansion with a hot über-rich playboy who could make her career? A miracle. Though she had no idea if Jack Brattle actually was a playboy. She could rule out gay now that she'd met him and had been on the receiving end of those eyes. If he was a playboy, he certainly kept his conquests as thoroughly out of the press as he kept himself. Maybe he sold his discarded women into slavery to ensure their silence.

She did think it was odd he wasn't more disconcerted about his door being left unlocked.

"Are you hungry?" He put a hand to his sadly now-covered stomach. "I'm starved. Hardly got a thing to eat tonight."

"Were you out?"

"For a while. The forecast convinced me to ring in the New Year at home."

"Considering the state of my car, you made the right choice. Home would have been a lot simpler."

And one-eighth the fun.

"Where in Philly is home?"

"Ah." She glanced pointedly at her surroundings. "A stunning three-room estate above a shoe-repair shop."

"Location, location, location."

"So they say. Did you grow up in this…hut?"

"Yes. You never did tell me if you were hungry."

"Famished." Another abrupt change of subject. He wasn't going to make this easy by volunteering long tales of his childhood, was he.

"This way to the kitchen." He pointed down the hall and curved his other arm behind her as if he were going to touch her, but ohh, not quite. "Or maybe you've already been there."

"I...took a peek, yes. Couldn't resist. This is so not my life."

"Don't assume that's a bad thing."

"No?" She turned at the top of the stairs to see his face. Reserved as usual. "Why? Most people would die to—"

"Most people have no idea."

Billionaire's Bitter Secret. "Tell me then."

"It's not what you think."

"What do you think I think?" She knew he thought she'd gone too far when he shot her a look and started down the stairs ahead of her. "You think I ask too many questions."

"You do sound like a reporter."

"Didn't I tell you I was one?" She laughed again, ha ha ha, watching him closely, but he only laughed, too, ha ha ha. Wow. Obviously he wasn't as suspicious as he seemed or he'd have been all over that one. "Just naturally curious I guess."

He ushered her into the kitchen and turned on subtle track lighting around the tops of the cabinets that lit the room one might almost say romantically, if one was thinking along those lines, but, of course, Hannah wasn't. She wasn't going to fall in the blink of an eye for any more toads who happened to be wearing prince's clothing. Might as well become infatuated with movie actors.

Of course, she did that, too.

"Have a seat." He indicated a tall stool pulled up to the space-age-looking island in the center of a vast area that would set any chef drooling, then rubbed his palms together. "What do you feel like?"

"Surprise me."

"Okay. Let's see." He narrowed his eyes, looked her up and down speculatively, which made her hope her stomach wasn't pooching out in doughy rolls. "You don't look like a peanut-butter-and-jelly woman..."

"Ha!" She put on a deeply offended look. "I'm a prime, grade A, number-one peanut-butter-and-jelly woman. My desert island food."

His smile made the corners of his deep brown eyes crinkle. "Then let's go in another direction. You game?"

"Sure." When he looked at her like that she'd agree to anything.

"Any foods you hate?"

"Tofu hot dogs. They taste like how my dentist's office smells."

He chuckled, which made him look twice as charming, she should mention, and worse, making him laugh gave her a stupid silly thrill. "Crossing tofu hot dogs off the list. Now…"

He looked around, as if choosing which cabinet to open and amaze her with first. Then he opened one with a flourish…and apparently struck out. As he did also on his second try. One more, and he made a sound of satisfaction and pulled out a couple of plates.

Hannah kept on her polite smile. He didn't know where he kept his plates? Did this man do nothing for himself? *Powerful Billionaire Helpless in His Own Home.*

Two drawers later he'd located knives, forks and spoons. Quite a while passed before he found champagne glasses. The champagne, however, he scored on his first try, and she'd just say that wow, it was not Asti Spumante, and it made her uncomfortable thinking of how much the bottle cost and how much her parents could have used the money she and…*Jack*…would drink up in such a short time. Probably a week's groceries in that bottle. Maybe two.

"To start us off." He removed the cork expertly and just as expertly poured her a glass. Clearly he had more experience with bartending than cooking, she'd guess with bottles exactly this expensive and more. "Happy New Year, Hannah."

"Thank you, Jack." She lifted her glass and toasted him, feeling a fizz of excitement even before she'd started drinking, a feeling she recognized all too well. No, no. No crushes. She was here as a professional first, not a female, and never the twain should meet. "You're not having any?"

"After I get the food ready."

"Cheers, then." She took her first sip tentatively, hoping to be able to sneer and assure herself a bottle of bubbles couldn't possibly be worth that much money.

Oh wow.

Not that she was an expert, in fact, she prided herself on being an expert on all things *not* likely to be in Jack Brattle's palace, but even she could tell the champagne was exquisite. Nothing like the swill Gerard served at the party, not that she'd blame him with that many people drinking that much. But this…tiny bubbles that streamed daintily upward, a smooth delicate flavor that changed over the course of the sip-swallow, and no sour aftertaste to ruin the experience. This was why champagne existed, and what everybody was after while making do with inferior stuff.

"I don't need to ask what you think, I can see it in your face."

"I was that obvious? How unchic of me. But, yes." She turned the glass reverently. "I'll have to work not to guzzle."

"Feel free." One eyebrow quirked. "I enjoy watching that much pleasure."

Ohh my. Except instead of arching an eyebrow back and saying something sultry like, *I'd love to show you exactly how much pleasure I can feel, Jack,* she gave a snort of nervous laughter and then made an even more revolting noise to get champagne out of her sinuses.

"You okay?"

"Mm, yeah. Sure. Fine." She thumped her chest and took another more cautious sip.

"I'll put the bottle where you can reach." He took a slim elegant wine cooler from under the island and slid the champagne inside, putting it on the counter next to her. "There's more where that came from."

"Thank you." There was more. More hundreds-of-dollars bottles of champagne. Not just this one, carefully saved for the occasion, of course not. The idea both thrilled and repelled her.

"Let's see what's in here." He rummaged through his refrigerator, mumbling to himself—which tickled her since she did the same thing—occasionally withdrawing cans or jars or various other containers, and placing them on the counter next to him. Hannah's bid to check out what billionaires had in their refrigerators besides not-Asti Spumante champagne was foiled when she couldn't stop checking out the pull of his wide shoulders under the soft-looking shirt and the shape of his beautiful you-know-what—yes, they were Lee jeans and, oh, he did such lovely things for them. They should be grateful. She certainly was.

A few minutes slicing this and that, arranging that and the other, another few minutes at the gleaming toaster, then he loaded up his haul onto a large lacquered tray and bore it triumphantly to the island. "Seems we've done pretty well."

"Um…yes." She put down her champagne and gaped. Suffice to say what was in his refrigerator bore absolutely no resemblance to what she had in hers. A glass jar of foie gras with slices of toasted brioche and thin slices of what looked like apple or pear but wasn't—maybe quince?; tins of osetra and beluga caviar to be served with delicate bone spoons alongside toasted pita bread squares, and a satiny white cream of some sort to spread over them; translucent slices of prosciutto next to a silver bowl of fresh green and black figs; cheeses whose names she didn't know on a polished elegantly grained wooden tray; olives in three colors; flawless miniature vegetables—tiny carrots, yellow squash, cucumbers and elongated radishes—with a green creamy herb dip; perfect maroon grapes the size of peas, tangerines the size of golf balls; plump raspberries whose gorgeous perfume made her want to bury her face in them; assorted miniature pastries…

"Are you expecting a crowd?"

"You said you were hungry."

"You eat like this all the time?"

He looked blank. "Doesn't everyone?"

Billionaire Out of Touch With Reality. She was about to roll her eyes when he winked, and she blushed instead, because the wink made it seem as if they were alone in a highly intimate situation. The fact that they *were* alone in a highly intimate situation only made her blush harder. But that wink would do it even in a crowd of thousands. And yet…how could she eat this? Enough for twenty people. What would he do with the leftovers? Toss them? To waste money and food…she hated the idea of both. However, no, she couldn't help herself. She was dying to try everything. Would he let her take some to share with Mom and Dad? With her friends. Her landlady? The whole block? Everyone should be able to eat like this.

"Now, the final touch." He fumbled with buttons on an under-cabinet music system and soft jazz floated into the room. Oh my. Oh my my my. You could absolutely not beat the cheesesteaks at Jake's Corner Bar, or the fresh almond cookies at Mama Fortunato's Bakery, or the sizzling shrimp at Hu Min's Dragon but…

Oh, but…

Mr. Amazing then rummaged in another three drawers before he found what he was looking for, which turned out to be candles. *Candles.* What kind of man thought of candles?

Perfection in a Male: My Evening with Jack Brattle.

Was this his typical evening at home? He couldn't have been expecting her. Maybe just a typical New Year's? But why would he haul it all out for her if he was planning a party later?

Was he…trying to *seduce* her?

She shouldn't, but with half a glass of excellent champagne in her, on top of a couple of glasses of not-so-excellent champagne, and dazzled by the man and the occasion, she sort of hoped so. Not that she could give in and sleep with *Jack Brattle* when she was planning to publish an article about him. She had her limits. What fun though to hold this memory close to her heart, and place it reverently into her best friends' voice mails and long e-mails to people she didn't know that well, for the rest of her life.

"Do you often throw impromptu candlelight suppers in the middle of the night for strange women?"

"I might make it a habit after tonight." He considered her carefully. "So far, no signs that you're a deranged killer…are you?"

"Ah, no. I gave up deranged killing. Hell on a girl's nails. And those dry-cleaning bills…" She made a tsk-tsk noise and shook her head.

"I hear you." He pulled up another stool close to hers, so what could she do but wiggle around until she faced him? "I'm glad you showed up."

"Really?" Fishing, fishing, she was shameless.

"Really." He poured himself champagne, topped hers off and put the bottle back in the fancy chill-thing, which undoubtedly kept it at the perfect temperature. "Since I left my party early, the evening didn't feel finished. I'm glad to have company to salvage it."

I Need a Woman: Billionaire's Sad Tale of Deprivation.

He clinked his glass to hers. "Dig in."

Maybe she shouldn't have, maybe she should have at least

hesitated and spent another minute or two contemplating the plight of the poor, but she didn't. She dug.

Oh my. Dug again. And again, and where was her shovel? If D. G. Jackson could see her, he'd never stop saying told-you-so. She'd deserve it, too.

"Caviar?" He passed it, amusement in his eyes.

Caviar…who knew? She'd had the jarred preserved stuff from the supermarket once and decided the fish should have been able to keep it.

"Foie gras?" The amusement became a smile.

Foie gras…she'd cheerfully gain forty pounds on the stuff given the chance.

"Prosciutto with figs?" This time he was outright smirking.

Prosciutto with fresh figs…sign her up for that action every day. And on and on, while they talked about the food she was eating: him discussing the various types of caviar, she bringing up overfishing in the Caspian Sea; he regaling her with memories of his first taste of foie gras, her mentioning the controversy involved in force-feeding the geese and ducks; him painting a picture of the summer he spent in Lebanon and the fig tree outside his bedroom window from which he could pick ripe figs first thing in the morning, to which she had no politically correct objections. All the while their champagne glasses were emptying and refilling until finally she couldn't eat or drink another bite and what a horrible shame that was.

"I have reached my absolute limit."

He drained the last of the bottle into her glass. "C'mon, I dare you."

"Oh, you Satan."

He picked up her practically licked-clean plate, grinning triumphantly. "Enjoyed it?"

"Ya think?" She gathered up dishes and bowls and placed

them in the sink. "I've never had a feast like that. I'm not much of a luxury foods person."

"Ah."

Something about the way he spoke made her glance at him suspiciously, though he was concentrating apparently innocently, on rinsing plates. What was that about? Had she disgraced herself with her greed? Maybe, but everything was so good she couldn't regret it. And he'd been eating quite healthily himself. Best of all, with Mr. Jack Brattle's notorious aversion to publicity, this multidollar-binge could remain her guilty secret.

"I feel like I should run about five miles to atone for those calories."

"There's a pool if you want to do laps."

Of course there was. "No suit."

"I'm sure you'd look great in one of mine…"

She giggled and blamed it on the champagne. "Um. Minor coverage problem."

"If you're sure…"

"No women in the house?" She tried to ask casually, and succeeded. She thought.

"Not for a long time."

"Are you divorced?" A natural question, wasn't it?

"No." He walked toward her, drying his hands.

"Never married?"

"Never. You?"

"Never. Girlfriend?"

"No. Boyfriend?"

"No."

And there they stood. If he was feeling anything like what she was feeling, the obvious circumstances of their proximity and their mutual singlehood were suggesting a number of delightful possibilities. Unfortunately there was that damn ethics thing because getting romantic with a man and then publishing an article about him was taking kissing and telling way further than she was comfortable taking it. But ohh, his mouth was so tempting, his lips full and sharply drawn, surrounded by the faint masculine gray of stubble-to-come.

A song came on, a smooth velvety jazz lullaby sung by a female artist whose voice she didn't recognize.

He took a step forward and she took one, too. His arms went up, one at her shoulder height, one at her waist. "Dance with me, Hannah."

Jack Brattle: All the Right Moves.

"Love to." Mmm, she hadn't been in a man's arms since Norberto, the smooth-tongued, talented-in-bed, charming, absolute cheating idiot creep jerk butthead...

Okay, she'd ignored all the warning signs and leapt happily into his arms and gotten her heart smacked down yet again. She should have known better.

But now, Jack Brattle smelled soooo good. And he moved like a dream. Under her hand, his shoulder was solid and warm, his chin also warm and smoothly close-shaven when it occasionally brushed her forehead. His fingers held hers lightly, but he kept his body close.

Hannah should know better right now. She'd have to crash down into reality all too soon. Somehow that seemed so deliciously far away, though, and he was so deliciously near.

"You dance divinely, Ms....what?"

"O'Reilly. Thank you. As do you, Mr....?"

She knew he wouldn't answer, but she lifted her head from where it had pillowed itself on the smooth comfortable front of his shirt and looked up expectantly.

"...Brattle." He stopped their dance. Looked down intently.

Her reaction was perfect, since she was actually shocked

and could do a convincing double take. She couldn't believe he'd told her. What about keeping himself such a tremendous secret all those years? All that trouble to stay hidden, and now he was telling her, a complete stranger who'd already joked she was a reporter and had been asking all kinds of questions?

Why would he do that?

Her treacherous imagination immediately supplied the kind of answer that was always getting her in trouble. Maybe he'd fallen for her, same as she'd fallen for him and therefore he had given her this incredible gift of trusting her with his identity.

She sighed. Nice story, but it never happened. At least not to her.

Something was definitely odd about the confession, but her brain discarded those thoughts because he was still inches away, their hands were still on each other's bodies, champagne fizzed through her veins, and since somewhere there must be someone for whom the name Jack Brattle rang only the faintest of bells, she decided the best possible course of action was to pretend to be that person, go on tiptoe and kiss him.

Of course, of *course* he kissed like a dream. The first was soft and quick, probably a surprised response to her typical lack of self-control. Then another at his initiation, longer and sweeter…then gradually hotter. Her body warmed, she felt his next kiss right down where kisses went when doled out by seriously sexy men. And when she pressed closer—and who could help it when his strong arms slid around her so completely—she could tell that he was…er, enjoying the kiss, too.

Mayday. She was completely crazed with lust, unbearably infatuated with everything about this man and this evening. This was where she should back up, think this through and make sure she understood every possible ramification of her—ooh.

He'd nudged her legs apart and put his thigh between hers,

which made her skirt ride upward. His hand dipped to caress her rear, which she faintly hoped, with the last glimmer of her sanity, had gotten firmer since she'd been going to the gym.

What had she been thinking? Something about pulling away. Something about…

Aw, hell.

He guided her back a few steps and lifted her onto the edge of his counter stool, stepped between her thighs and kissed her exactly how women all over the world longed to be kissed whether they knew it or not. He was very hard now, pushing the swollen heat against her thin, red, lace panties, making her nearly ready to come just thinking about being in bed with him.

Wasn't she supposed to stop this? Something about a story, about ethics…

His lips left hers to explore her neck; his hands drew her skirt slowly up, building her arousal with the expectation of more intimate touch. He slid those same warm hands back and forth on her hips as more and more of her skin became available to his fingers.

Must…hang on…to brain. "Jack."

"Mmm."

"This is a little…unreal."

"How so?"

"You and this amazing house and the incredible food and the champagne and now…this."

"What 'this'?"

"Nothing that should be happening." Her voice was low and breathless, making it damn clear how serious she was about stopping. Which would be not enough.

"I know. It's a lousy idea."

"You do? It is?" She opened her eyes. "Why shouldn't you be doing it?"

"Shh. Pretend it's not happening." He trailed his fingers

across the lower edge of her abdomen, then along the lacy sides of her panties. "What happens tonight stays there. In the morning, it will all be erased."

"So…this isn't happening?"

"No." He urged her legs farther apart, slid fingers teasingly inside the lace edge. "It's not happening."

"Mmm, Jack, but it…really does feel like it's happening." She braced her feet on the chair rungs, lifted her hips. He took his cue and slid her panties down, got them over one leg and let them fall down the other.

"No, don't worry." He knelt and she leaned her elbows behind her on the counter, tipped her head back, open and vulnerable to him, feeling his warm breath on her sex, closing her eyes in delicious impatience for his even warmer tongue. "I promise it's not happening."

"If you say so—*oh!*" She gasped, let her hips lift and retreat under his talented thrusts, so close to coming so soon that she had to take deep breaths and open her eyes to slow the process down. She wanted him with her. She wanted this to last forever. But, no, she wasn't going to hold out much longer. "Are you sure this isn't happening? It really *really* feels like it is. Any second now."

"Let it happen, Hannah."

"I want you with me."

"I don't have a condom downstairs."

"But if this isn't happening…" She was panting, trying desperately to hold on to some kind of logic. "Then we don't need…oh!"

He'd moved to kiss her inner thighs, but now settled firmly back on her clit and she was lost. The orgasm started in a dark rush, then boom, steam engine blowing past, making everything rattle and roll in its wake, subsiding eventually to the distance and the past.

"Oh my goodness." She slowly unclenched her muscles, slumped wearily back on the counter, staring at him with what was certainly a worshipful look as he stood up, smiling male triumph.

Then the impact of what she'd just done hit nearly as hard as the orgasm, creating a serious rupture in her afterglow. Sex with an interviewee who didn't know yet that he was an interviewee…absolutely not. He'd think she'd slept with him for the story.

Jack Brattle—*Jack Brattle*—stepped forward and scooped her back to upright, bent and kissed her hard, once, then again and nearly overwhelmed her dismayed and blissful heart by gazing into her eyes and smoothing back what must by now be a rat's-nest hairdo. "You know they say what happens to you New Year's Day predicts how you'll spend your whole year?"

"Does it?" She smiled wistfully up at him, already in love with this perfect, beautiful, incredibly talented-tongued man. "Then this is going to be the best year of my life."

"I haven't had a perfect night like this in a long time."

Something about how he said it made her think that instead of being polite, he meant the words literally. "Me, neither."

She meant them literally, too.

"I have a brilliant idea." He held out his hand. "Come upstairs with me and we'll make more things not happen."

"That *is* a brilliant idea." Hannah accepted his hand, slid off the stool, picked up her panties and took a moment to get her hips working while he supported her. "As soon as I can walk again."

Up the stairs, then, resting her fingers in his, anticipation mixing with dread, mixing with elation, mixing with sadness. Maybe none of this would have happened by morning as far as he was concerned, but she doubted she'd ever forget a single second.

Not only that, but morning was going to come way too soon. And with it the dismal certainty that once again she'd done plenty of leaping without the slightest bit of looking beforehand. And once again she'd have to pay—this time by having to give up the career opportunity of a lifetime.

4

HE WAS SO SCREWED. NO MATTER how he played the rest of this evening, Derek was screwed. Everything had gone as planned, but nothing was working out as it should.

Obviously Dee-Dee had played her role perfectly at Gerard Banks's party, dangling the Jack Brattle interview in front of Hannah and supplying her with directions to the house. He'd had no doubt she'd take the bait. However, once the weather had changed so dramatically for the worse, he'd never dreamed she'd risk driving out tonight. After his shower earlier in the evening, he'd been about to relock the gate and front door.

Instead, he'd met Hannah for the first time stark naked. That hadn't been part of the plan. Nor had been his immediate attraction, which only compounded the interest and curiosity that was sparked by the provocative wit she revealed in her Lowbrow column, blogs and occasional features in *The Philadelphia Sentinel*.

He'd started the Highbrow column as D. G. Jackson when Philly's restaurant scene began to take off, wanting to indulge his passion for food on the one hand, and on the other, wanting to introduce the average man and woman to dishes, flavors and establishments he or she might otherwise be intimidated by. In his view, good food was one of life's greatest joys. But once Hannah began countering his "highbrow" suggestions with her "lowbrow" alternatives, he quickly learned that she knew what she was talking about as well as he did. He took great pleasure in going—incognito, of course—to every hole-in-the-wall and mom-and-pop joint she recommended, all of which satisfied as she promised.

His interest only intensified along with their public rivalry. Who was Hannah O'Reilly? What was she like? How could he find out? He wouldn't call her an obsession, but he certainly thought about her more than was normal, certainly more than any woman he'd met since he'd been forced by circumstances in his early twenties to grow up practically overnight. Okay, maybe obsessed. But not being the kind of man who tolerated unanswered questions, he'd come up with tonight's plan.

The chance for Hannah to experience the lifestyle of the elusive Jack Brattle was his bait. Lure hungry journalist with promises of the interview of a lifetime, then make her the most "highbrow" meal he could whip up, secretly document her enjoyment, and in his last column before he left Philadelphia for good, skewer her as a closet gourmet. Anyone with taste buds as unerring as hers would be an easy mark.

Hannah had shown up, Derek played the Suspicious Heir act apparently convincingly and she'd gone down without a fight—though he wished he could have captured photographic evidence of her shoving in the foie gras and washing it down ecstatically with Pol Roger Cuvée Sir Winston Churchill 1985.

After the "impromptu" meal, perfectly poised for a wrap to the ultimate checkmate, what did he do? He asked her to dance. Nice one. What did he think, he'd have her gorgeous body pressed against his and remain completely impassive, then *Hey, thanks for the dance, I'm off to bed, choose a room, and see you in the morning?* He'd immediately started getting ideas involving a lot more than dancing, fueled wilder when it became apparent she was getting the same ones.

Now…with this beautiful, sexy, willing woman stranded in his house, to say that things had gotten out of hand was like saying winter got chilly in Antarctica. Lure her, yes, feed her, yes, dance with her…okay. Kiss her? Bad idea. Succumb to the sexual promise of her blue eyes, rose lips and slender body?

He'd already said he was screwed.

Worse, he was leading her upstairs, unsatisfied lust driving out common sense. Once she got into his bedroom…

Well, *she'd* be screwed. He didn't want to think about how low this was for him to go. He might be fascinated by Hannah way beyond the typical male interest in boobs and a great ass, but nothing he could say would convince her of that if she knew who he was and why she was here.

His only hope of going through with the rest of the night without feeling like total scum was to ditch the idea of the article. At least she hadn't admitted yet that she was a reporter, so he wasn't the only one holding back truths. Granted, she'd dipped a cautious toe in honesty, but quickly gave up total immersion when he pretended to think she was joking.

What a pair. *I'll lie to you, you lie to me, come into bed, and we'll lie together.*

He got to the end of the hall, pushed open the dark door— so much dark in this house to accompany the dark memories—pulled her into the room and into his arms. She nestled against him; he lowered his chin onto her hair, inhaling her light perfume, more tropical and exotic than he would have expected on a woman whose face could be in an Ivory soap commercial…and whose body could be in an X-rated movie—okay, the perfume made sense.

Either way, Ivory or triple X, she was driving him wild.

Watching her come… He was going to have to do some serious soul-searching if he wanted his ego to regain control of his id.

Did he? He wasn't sure. Because the alternative would be very, very sweet.

"So…" She drew back, keeping her hands linked lightly behind his neck. "What's not going to happen now?"

Oh, the choice of words. If he had any sense of honor, he'd tell her everything wasn't going to happen now, he was D. G. Jackson, he'd set her up for this entire evening, though he hadn't planned the sexual part, and—

"Hmm?" She started rotating her pelvis seductively against his erection.

"Hannah."

"Ye-e-es?"

"I can't think while you're doing that."

"Do you need to?"

Yes. He needed to. But thought wouldn't be easy. Hell, it might not even be possible. Her lips were parted, eyes half-closed, head tipped back as she gazed at him. Her skin was so smooth, her neck so long and graceful, the clingy dress sparkled and winked at him so enticingly…

"I'm thinking that—"

"No." She moved forward again; her tongue painted a short line on his throat, then she closed her lips over the moisture in a brief biting kiss that made him want to pick her up, throw her on the bed and visit heaven. "Don't think, Jack. Just do…me."

Her whisper made him groan. He couldn't take advantage of her like this. Someday in some form even though he was leaving *The Herald,* she might find out what D. G. Jackson looked like and loathe him forever. Either he told her right now, or—

She let go of his neck abruptly, backed up a few steps, reached to the hem of her dress and pulled it slowly up.

Oh, no. No no no. If she did that, he was—

Long thighs came into view, widening into round hips un-interrupted by the red lace panties that unhinged him earlier. A curving female waist, full breasts barely contained in a red lace demibra.

—lost. He was lost.

The dress dangled from her triumphant fingers, then dropped. She arched her soft brown brows. "What are you thinking now?"

"Ungh." His caveman grunt made her laugh. To hell with it. Buy now, pay later. He'd make love to her until she begged him to stop, have her sign an I'll-never-tell document she'd assume typical of Jack Brattle, have her towed home as soon as the weather cooperated and change his planned final Highbrow article. He'd be selling the house soon. Hannah would never meet D. G. Jackson or Jack Brattle in person. Or maybe if she ever did, by then she'd think this was funny.

Right. Maybe.

The plan had flaws wide enough to drive a Hummer through, but with a half-drunk horny woman wearing nearly nothing—no, with *this particular* half-drunk horny woman wearing nearly nothing, anything sounded better than turning her down.

"You have on too many clothes." He shrugged clumsily out of his shirt, yanked his undershirt over his head, still uneasy over his lame justification. Where was his nobility?

"I was so hoping that's what you were thinking." She put her hands to the back of her bra.

To hell with nobility. Nobility would leave him more frus-trated tonight than he'd probably ever been in his life. The promise of those breasts…

"No." He waggled his finger at her, the stern taskmas-ter. "My job."

"Yes, sir." Her arms fell to her sides. Her sexy mouth, crimson lipstick by now only a faint hue, looked all the more tempting for the smile that spread it. "Your job."

He'd never make it. He'd get within an inch of her, and he'd come just from that smile. Out of his jeans, impatiently out of his briefs, he strode toward her, stopping inches away, not coming, but more than ready to start trying.

"Make it all not happen, Jack. All of it." She spoke with earnest passion. "Any way you want it not to happen works for me."

He grinned, slowly, enjoying her humor, her obvious eagerness. The last woman he'd made love to had the body of a Playboy Bunny and the brain of a squid. Suffice to say, he'd had too much to drink that night and been embarrassingly desperate for sexual contact. But Hannah was Hannah, and he wanted this to be good even if it was going to be their one and only night together. Even if they were both lying through their teeth about who they really were. At least they were honest about wanting this.

What a way to meet.

His hands found her waist, followed her smooth firm lines back and around, wandered up her undulating spine-trail to the closure of her bra. He unhooked it slowly, his eyes anticipating the glorious moment of her full breasts' release from the confining lace.

Ohh, man. The thought of being able to see this body naked only this one time made him want to weep.

And the thought took him aback. With women these days he was absorbed only in the erotic present. No emotions had been involved since his first girlfriend, Amy, back in college, before his father's life shattered and brought his mother's down with it. How often and how deeply he traced losses back to that hellish year. Loss of trust, loss of the desire and capacity for true intimacy. Was it possible to break the cycle if the right woman came along?

~~Derek pushed the thoughts away.~~ *Lighten up, dude,* as his Oberlin roommate would say. It was New Year's Eve, he'd been seduced by champagne and this woman, with all her possibilities. By morning, she'd have to be another brief conquest like the rest of them. In the meantime…he'd give her what they both wanted before he disappeared.

He lifted her and set her down on the edge of his bed, savoring the way her arms came around him to help support her weight. Starved for female touch, he knelt to worship her body, rubbing his cheek around each heavy breast, glad he'd shaved to spare her feeling sandpaper. Her scent was exquisite, the voluptuous softness of her skin enticing, the smooth weight against his face thrilling. Her nipples responded to his tongue and teeth; she moaned and didn't resist when he pushed her gently back on the quilt-covered mattress and climbed over her, settling between her legs, not entering yet, though his cock was in a frenzy. Too soon. He wanted this to last forever. As if anything could.

She pushed her hands up the columns of his arms, met his eyes unwillingly, hers unexpectedly shy and vulnerable. "Hi."

"Hi." He was undone by those eyes, suddenly and fiercely protective of her, naked underneath him, opening herself willingly to a stranger. Crazy old-fashioned idea. For all he knew, she spread for every guy she met. Boatloads of them a week. Though he didn't think so, didn't know why not, just instinct, about the only thing he trusted anymore.

"This is still not happening, right?"

Suddenly he felt a longing so fierce it startled him. He kissed her forehead, her cheeks, then her mouth, long lingering kisses, hoping the vulnerability he'd glimpsed in her eyes meant she felt the same.

"Nope. Not happening."

"Whew. Good."

Yeah. Great. He reached for a condom from his night table to hide the surge of anger he recognized as disappointment in her reaction, then settled back over her. If he kept his brain on tits, ass and pussy, he'd be fine.

Except he wanted much more out of this night with her, all the more so since it would be their only one together. So he took his time, tasted her mouth leisurely, willing her to be seduced by his lips and tongue until she wanted this to be "not happening" as much as he did. She responded warmly, her arms encircling his shoulders. His hand wandered to her breast; he slid his palm back and forth, brushing her nipple gently side to side. Her kisses grew hotter; her hands clenched in his hair. Triumph swelled. Her control was wavering. She wanted him as much as he wanted her. And he wanted her more apparently than he wanted his own integrity intact.

His erection found her sex, barely nudged into her opening, forward, back, forward, back, no more than half an inch. Her legs spread; her hips lifted; she made an impatient sound. Still he teased, press, release, press, release.

She wrapped one arm around his back, brought her knees up beside his shoulders, reached down and spread herself wide with her fingers. "Jack."

"Something you wanted?"

"Um." She gave a short hoarse laugh. "Yeah."

"What's that?" He whispered the words in her hair, lifted his hips to give his hand access to the sweet moisture between her legs, trailing his fingers up and down her sex, loving the way she hissed in breath when he lingered over her clitoris. She was so responsive. So uninhibited. He wanted to believe she was like this only with him.

"Er… I find that sex is a lot better…" Hiss of incoming

breath. He slid a finger inside her and she gasped the air out again. "When you actually have it."

"Really." He wasn't going to be able to hold back much longer. The calm and cool act would be completely blown if she could feel his heart thudding, hear the lust-roaring of his too-long denied body. She was so beautiful. "Interesting idea."

"Do it. Now." She took hold of his cock and guided it straight where it most wanted to be, wriggling her hips up and around, trying deliciously to impale herself.

His control vaporized; he lowered and let his muscles do the work they were so desperate to do, sliding into her as gradually as he could manage, trying not to dwell on the smooth tight feel of her gripping his length or he'd come too soon.

Her blissful sigh nearly undid him.

"Like that?"

"Mmm, like that."

He moved slowly, against all instincts urging him to pump until his orgasm had its way, made sure he stimulated her, concentrated on making her as crazy for him as he was for her.

She fell in with his rhythm, her body flushing, her eyes glazed and sensual. He had to look away. She was too perfect. Too beautiful. Too close and too intimate like this. His chest ached dangerously; he wanted, insanely, to possess her in a far more lasting way than just this one night.

In defense, he closed his eyes, sped his rhythm, trying to finish before he lost his heart—or his mind. He wasn't sure which was in danger, maybe both. She whimpered, and he tried to block out the sound, wanting her over the edge ahead of him. Her legs locked around his back; her head made swishing noises on his pillow; her breath grew rapid and hoarse. He loved what he was doing to her. He wanted to do this to her every day; he didn't want another man touching her ever, no one ever making her feel like this but him.

Tension locked her body; he opened his eyes so he could watch the ecstasy on her face as he felt her pulsing around his cock. Her cheeks were pink, lips parted, expression awed and blissful.

His own climax tore through him; at its peak he joined their mouths and kissed her with every shred of passion he could feel, more than he knew possible.

Then it was over. Lost, he rolled them to one side, still inside her, gathered her to him, his chin resting on her hair, listening to their breathing gradually slow, feeling their hearts still pounding.

He'd been a fool to think he could make love to this woman and call it over. He wanted more. He wanted to talk to her every day, eat with her every day, to make her laugh, give her everything she wanted and things she didn't even know she wanted.

Where had these emotions come from? How had he gone from seeing sex as an occasional human necessity with whomever appealed, to wanting to devour everything about this woman? Had she drugged him? Bewitched him? Had he become such an emotional hermit that the need in him exploded retroactively? He didn't know.

But he had to tell her at least some of the truth or nothing more than tonight would be possible. After the power of what just passed between them, maybe she could forgive and forget…and want more, as well.

Though no doubt his confession would make for a rough few hours.

"Hey." She stretched and started stroking and massaging his neck and shoulders, making him want to handcuff her to his bed so she could do the same every night.

"Mmm?"

"That was incredible."

"It was certainly that."

"And totally unexpected."

"Totally." He caught her hand, kissed her fingers and set them back down to continue their magic. "You should get lost in more snowstorms."

"I should, if they lead me to you." Her hands worked their way up onto his scalp. Pure heaven. "You said other women showed up to seduce you. Did you ever take advantage?"

"Never."

"Really?"

"I guess you caught me in a moment of weakness."

"Which you now regret."

He chuckled. "Not in a million years."

"Did any of them know who you were?"

"Some might have suspected."

"Jack…" Something in her tone kept him from the complete relaxation her fingers promised. "Why did you tell me your last name?"

Derek shrugged, not sure why he'd carried it that far himself. "You asked."

"But you've been hiding from the world for so long."

"You're not the world."

"Seriously." She stopped her magic, got up on one elbow to see his face. "How do you know I won't go out there and tell everyone where you are?"

He didn't like this turn to the conversation at all. He winked and gave her an über-villain stare. "Because, my schveet-haht, you vouldn't enjoy ze consequences."

She giggled, looking slightly nervous. "Tell me you're kidding."

"Ah, Hannah. Let's not go into it." Her apparent excitement

about Jack Brattle made him uneasy. She was a reporter after all… "Instinct told me I could trust you. Let's leave it at that."

"Okay." She smiled and snuggled against him, her body molded to his, head fitting comfortably on his shoulder. "I'm glad you trust me."

He did. Implicitly. But he wasn't going to ask if she trusted him. Because he couldn't bear to hear that she did, knowing how much he was betraying that trust. He needed to tell her. He would…

But right now she was so warm against him, and the room felt so peaceful and complete while outside the storm still buffeted the house. His eyes were getting heavy. Her breathing had already slowed.

Later. There was time for truth later…

He didn't know how long he'd slept but couldn't be bothered to lift his head and check the clock. Light was showing around the edges of his shades. Late morning? Early afternoon? A rush of wind drove sleet against the windows. Good. The snow was still raging. Hannah would have to stay. They'd have time to argue out his confession, let the anger settle, and then…?

She stirred against him, her soft thigh came across the top of his. His cock responded. She made a small sound and stirred again. He followed the line of her back with his fingers, over the curve of her firm and fantasy-fulfilling ass, and into the crevasse, stroking the sensitive area gently.

"Mmm. G'morning."

Her voice made him smile. Her body made him hard. He respected her brain, admired her spirit, loved her humor. Was there anything else before he found himself in too deep?

He turned on his side, adjusted her thigh over him, reached for the condom he'd stashed under his pillow, just in case, then got busy making sure she was as turned on as he was. She kept her eyes closed, but her body responded with motions, whimpers, moisture between her legs. He still held off, teasing her, listening for her breathing to gauge what she liked best. When she finally opened her eyes pleadingly, he knew. How many women had he been able to understand this well this soon? Not many. Maybe not any.

Inside her, he started a sleepy rhythm to match their moods, gripping her hips to give him control. Slow and sweet. The perfect way to start a—

She pushed hard, rolled him over to his back, climbed on and started riding, pinning his wrists to the mattress with her weight, her heavy breasts swinging, her skin gradually flushing, strong thighs working on either side of his body.

Oh, man. "This isn't tiring you?"

"At the moment—" she arched her back, panting, ground her pelvis against him, then rode harder "—I don't care."

The way she was making him feel, her insistent rhythm, the triple X sight of her made him almost not care, either. Almost.

He freed his hands, put them to her hips to help her along, try to keep some of the pressure off her legs. "Are you sure you—"

"I'm sure." She accepted his help, raised her arms over her head, eyes closed, breasts bouncing, stomach pulled taut. It was too much.

"Hannah." He gritted his teeth.

She put one arm down, found her clitoris and started adding to her own pleasure.

He lifted his hands, cupped the beautiful rounds of her breasts. The feel of her warm flesh in his palms, the sight of her face flushed with desire sent him over the edge. He grabbed her hips again, practically lifted off the bed with the force of his orgasm.

His beautiful, ethereal porn queen gasped; her fingers sped; she gasped again, then opened her eyes and looked into his as he felt her contracting.

There was no way, no way, this one day with her, this one incredible night with her, was going to be remotely enough. Why the hell, when her articles and blogs had intrigued him so much, hadn't he just called her and asked her out? Why put them both through this elaborate and underhanded charade? Had he gotten so used to not trusting people, to approaching them with suspicion after his father's betrayal, that he couldn't even ask a girl he was interested in out to dinner?

Something told him this time with Hannah was going to change his life. He wasn't sure how, or whether his future would involve her still, but he knew he wouldn't be the same after this experience. He'd make sure of it.

She collapsed onto him. He waited until they could both breathe more normally, then rolled her carefully back next to him. "You okay?"

"More than okay." Her voice was languorous, sated. He wanted her to feel that all the time. But only if it was because of him. "Tremendously okay."

"You're amazing, Hannah."

"No, you."

He chuckled, stroking her hair, wishing again there was another way they could have met.

"Jack."

The name stabbed into his happiness. He still had a small matter to clear up. "Mm?"

"Now that you have given my body more pleasure than it has ever had with food and incredible sex, it's time to get down to business."

"Business?" He didn't like that word. "What do you mean?"

"I want you to tell me more about you." She put a possessive hand on his chest. "I want to know everything about Jack Brattle. Absolutely everything."

Derek stopped stroking. Dread started leaching away the afterglow. She couldn't be— Not after what they'd shared. "Dull stuff, all of it."

"I'm sure it's fascinating." She lifted her head, eyes alight. "Tell me. Your life, your childhood, your job, everything. Pretend I'm…oh, I don't know…"

"Going to write an article about me?"

Her face froze, then fell. "No. I…no. Of course not."

Derek disentangled himself and sat up abruptly. "Back in a minute."

In the bathroom, he wrapped the condom in a tissue, tossed it into the garbage, ran hot water onto a washcloth and cleaned himself off. Cleaned her off of him. He was a fool. Hannah had slept with him as Jack Brattle in order to get a story.

What kind of naive idiot had he been? He'd set her up for the sake of his own story, but he'd cancelled that plan after what happened between them. Now looky here, she'd set him up, too. Pouring on the charm, not asking too many questions too early, waiting for after the big seduction when she'd hooked him and her curiosity would seem more natural.

He should have realized she'd do anything to get the scoop. He'd been so smug about his clever trump-card joke, so egocentric once it backfired, thinking only of how she made him feel and how much he wanted her. He hadn't been thinking of her motives. What a sick joke, arrogantly assuming he was as irresistible to her as she was to him. Worse, for a man as cynical as he was, he'd assumed she felt the strong pull between them and had fallen under its spell to the same degree he had. Apparently that strong pull was pure fantasy on his part, born of reading too many of her columns and imagining in a too-lonely life that they'd share a connection. Not much better than a kid with a celebrity crush.

An interview with the infamous Jack Brattle. The big prize, the brass ring. Sex was merely the means. Derek wasn't a man, he was a stand-in for a celebrity scoop, a pawn in her quest for the story to launch her career.

A story he was about to bring to a swift and unhappy ending.

5

HE WAS *WHO?*

This was not happening. This was so not happening. This was so completely not—

Again with the "not happening"? This horror *was* happening. And it made her wish the sex hadn't. Except rolling around in the sheets with…this man…was so amazing, that Hannah had convinced herself she was hours away from falling irrevocably for…someone she thought was someone else.

Not again, this pain and disappointment in matters of the heart. Not again! And yet…what did she expect going instantly gaga over a complete stranger?

"So…you're actually D. G. Jackson?"

"Yes." He stared at her moodily.

"Not Jack Brattle."

He kept staring. She could not get her brain around this at all. She'd just spent one of the best nights of her life—and had the best first-time sex of her life—with D. G. Jackson, the columnist. *Not* Jack Brattle, the billionaire.

It made no sense. What was D. G. Jackson doing in Jack Brattle's house, besides seducing her under an assumed identity? And why instead of looking like an abashed sinner now, was he giving *her* a contemptuous sneer as if she'd somehow tricked *him?* In an incredibly vile and disgraceful way, she might add.

Oh, this hurt. Horribly. Were men ever who they seemed? Ever, ever, *ever?*

Worse, she was so wonderfully naked alone with him three minutes ago, and now he had on black silk boxers, and she wanted nothing more than to grab his—or whoever's—sheets from the bed, cover herself and go fetal on the floor, whimpering. But she didn't want to show any weakness. Didn't want him to see how much he'd hurt her. All she wanted was to rise from the bed and with considerable dignity, set his pubic hair on fire.

"Would you mind telling me what the hell is going on?"

"I set you up." He spoke matter-of-factly, as if he tricked people into his bed every day of the week, which was entirely possible. "Dee-Dee is a friend of mine."

"Dee-Dee." She could barely gasp out the syllables. This was…odious! A supremely sick joke, except D.G.—*D.G.!*—wasn't laughing. He didn't look as if he enjoyed this at all. Which made two of them. "You tricked me into thinking you were Jack Brattle."

How ghastly. How low and vicious and mean. She wasn't sobbing with rage only because shock still held her rigid.

"Yes, I did." He didn't sound anything but angry.

Luckily she'd already suffered the loss of the Brattle interview since *she* had principles that prevented her from acting like a slimebag butthead, or she'd want to run outside and beg another branch to fall, this time on her. Or, hell, why not just order one up for a crash landing on the head of D. G. Jackson?

"What are you doing in Jack Brattle's house?"

"The house is mine."

"*Yours.*" She was hopelessly confused. He said that as if she *had* really trespassed instead of showing up at his Jack Brattle-worthy mansion exactly as he intended she should. And what the hell kind of salary did *The Philadelphia Herald* pay, anyway? "So Jack Brattle…"

"Is completely out of the picture."

No Jack Brattle. Just D. G. Jackson, a newspaper columnist with a mansion and apparently a Paul Bunyan-sized ax to grind with her. Had he really been that put out by Grey Poupon? It was excellent mustard. "Why did you do this?"

"The meal you ate downstairs was going to be the subject of my next Highbrow piece. *Lowbrow Columnist is Closet Gourmet.*"

Her face grew hot. The room looked wrong, too bright or something. A weird high pitch played in her ears. She didn't think she'd *ever* been this furious. Not even with another man. She was a good sport. Objectively she could see the humor in the situation. She could see how luring her to eat everything her column was opposed to would be a really good score.

Except for one rather overwhelming detail.

"You *slept* with me. Was that going in the article, too? Any hidden cameras for pictures you're planning to run with the column?"

"No." He glanced away, the first sign that he might be feeling at least some guilt over what he'd done. Thank God. She was beginning to think he was a sociopath.

"That's why you were so insistent anything physical between us 'wasn't happening.' I get it. How practical. Just delete the inconvenient aspects of responsibility and still get what you want." She bounced off the bed to avoid the pain of sitting there feeling sick and rejected, made a futile grab for her panties, missed them through her tears, and had to lunge for them again.

"You were willing to screw Jack Brattle for a story."

His flat accusation stopped her. She gaped at him, panties dangling from her clenched fingers. Screw Jack Brattle for a story? Ha! If only she'd been smart enough to do it for that reason. But, no. She'd started out wanting the story, but ended up wanting only him. Because he was funny and sexy and charming and had set the stage for one of the most wonderful and romantic nights of her life. Because in spite of his wealth making him stand for everything she'd been brought up not to value, he'd gotten under her skin and, while he was inside her body, also into her heart. Because she was an idiot, but okay, no point belaboring that.

Afterward, she'd been greedy to know everything about him, to absorb his background, likes, dislikes, routines, hobbies, no longer for a story—because how could she publish anything after sleeping with him?—but to immerse herself in him, to draw them closer so her knowledge could catch up at least partway to her feelings.

When would she learn?

So he'd taken her questions about him as a sign she could play dirty, too. Fine. She wasn't stupid enough to show more vulnerability now. "What's it to you who I screw or why?"

"Nothing." He shrugged carelessly. "It's nothing to me either way."

"Super." She yanked the panties right side out, wondering how much more pain she could stand before she split in half from the pressure. "Well, thanks for the orgasms. I've gotta go."

He gestured toward the ice-covered window. "Out in that?"

"Nothing—" she nearly lost her balance when her toes tangled in red lace "—is going to keep me from leaving this house."

"Without a car? You'll freeze to death."

"If you want to be concerned over my welfare, you should turn back time and rethink some of this disgusting little trick you pulled last night.'

"Ah, right. Just one question."

"What." Panties finally on, she jammed her hands on her hips, then realized she was still topless and crossed her arms over her chest.

"When were you planning to tell Jack you were a reporter? After you left his bed and published his life story?"

In her outrage she forgot to keep her breasts covered and had to hug herself again. "*How* hypocritical. *You* set me up from the beginning to get a story under false pretenses. I fell into this situation. And I actually did tell him—you—that I was—am—a reporter."

His eyebrows lifted.

"Okay, only sort of, but I did." She looked around for her bra, kicking herself for not realizing that's why he let the ha-ha joke about her job pass so easily, when anyone as vulturously protective of his privacy as Jack Brattle wouldn't have let her get away with even the most obvious lie about it. Nor would he have admitted who he was in the first place. She'd noticed and wondered, yet she wanted so desperately to believe in the fantasy, just like she always wanted to believe in fantasy and romance and fairy tales and probably even Santa Claus if her bratty cousin Tom hadn't burst that particular bubble. A career-catapulting interview with a sexy billionaire who couldn't help falling desperately in love with her and she with him? Are you kidding? Who could resist that?

Get real, Hannah. Not even in the movies did they make stories that fantastic.

"Anyway, D.G., you—"

"Derek."

"What?"

"My name is Derek."

"You're changing it again?"

His expression didn't waver. "It's Derek."

"Fine. *Derek.* Whatever. You knew I was a reporter when

we slept together. I didn't know you weren't Jack. And what kind of life story was I going to publish when you don't even have the right life?"

"That's not the point."

"It is to me." She found her bra sticking halfway under the bed, put it on inside out and had to take it off again, turning her back when she noticed Derek's—*Derek's, not Jack's*—eyes lingering on her breasts, which, in spite of her one-hundred-degrees-in-the-shade rage, remembered his touch and wanted more.

Super. She'd reached a new low in falling for lowlifes. *The more they abuse me, the harder I fall. Humiliate me. Trick me. Lie to me. I'm yours, baby, and keep up the pain.*

"You can't go anywhere in this weather, Hannah."

"Try and stop me." She snatched her dress off the floor and jammed it over her head, not caring if it ended up wrong-way around. Her shoes were downstairs, her coat was in the—

Hands landed on her shoulders; she ducked and whirled to face him. "What are you doing?"

"Trying to stop you."

"Do me a favor and don't do anything else to me for the rest of your life."

He put his hands on his hips and regarded her darkly. Which of course made him look intense and masculine and even more gorgeous than he did looking cheerful, which was already too gorgeous for her sanity. "What's the plan, walking the rest of the day through an ice storm?"

"Give me a phone, I'll call Triple A."

"No phones."

"Oh, be serious." She scanned the furniture and walls, tried to remember one in any of the rooms she'd been in. "What is this, *The Shining?*"

"It's a cell-only house."

She didn't buy that for a microsecond. "Then give me your cell."

"Gee." He crossed his arms over his broad, bare, fantasy-perfect chest. "I forget where it is."

"I thought you'd want me to leave."

"I don't want your death on my conscience."

"But my humiliation is resting there quite comfortably?"

"Hannah…" Was it her imagination or had his voice become slightly conciliatory? "The joke was meant to be just that. A joke."

"Once you slept with me it became very not funny."

"Sex was not part of the plan." His voice had definitely gentled. "And trust me, that part was no joke."

Oh, no. She fought against the warm fuzzies and the stupid, *stupid* hope. She'd never learn. "What was it, then?"

"It was…" He rubbed his hand over his forehead, looking suddenly tired, which made her anger ebb further and her desire rise to put him to bed and give him a backrub. Honestly! She should still be wanting to kick him where it counted. "Let's call it the intersection of attraction, opportunity and good champagne."

"Ah." She took in a huge breath and let it out quickly. She had to stop listening to him right now. Because once he started, he'd make it all sound so reasonable. How often had she been through this… She'd listen, empathize with everything from his point of view, see how she was partly if not mostly at fault and forgive him. In the process, once again she'd forget that her needs and emotions had been completely left out of the equation. How often had she done that? Too many times to count. No more. No more. Neither of them had acted with impeccable integrity, however in her book he'd crossed a much bigger line than she had, and she wasn't going to play forgiving doormat anymore.

"I'll need a crowbar."

Very understandably he looked startled. "For my skull?"

"For my car windows. So I can get my own phone."

"Uh, fresh out of crowbars."

"I'll find something." She glanced around. A couple of porcelain lamps, which would shatter. She wasn't quite up to throwing a bureau or his king-size bed. Her mind went over the house's layout. Fireplace poker? There must be one. She headed for the door.

"You can't be serious."

"If you say so." Out of the room, she jogged down the hall—Derek G. Jackson's hall, damn him all to hell—down the steps, not hearing any furious signs of pursuit and feeling oddly triumphant and disappointed at the same time.

In the living room, as she grabbed, yes, a poker, she heard him at the top of the stairs and rushed to jam on her damp high heels, longing for the gray fuzzy-lined boots sitting in her apartment's front hallway. No time for a coat. She'd run out and bash the window, grab her phone, and call for help in getting away ASAP from Mr. Not-Jack-Brattle.

She flung the front door open. The cold and wind hit her like an air bag. Ice crystals stung. Hannah stopped on the threshold. This was stupid, wasn't it. Another Harebrained Hannah move. But what choice did she have, other than to sacrifice her pride by crawling back inside and staying until the storm abated? If she couldn't retrieve the phone, she could lock herself in his bathroom or something equally mature.

This was awful.

Over the wind she barely heard feet thudding down the stairs. "Hannah, for God's sake, don't be an idiot."

That did it. Out the front door, closing it behind her. Wobbling across the front stoop. One step down the staircase and she hit ice. Her foot twisted. Slipped.

Bam. Bam. Bam. Down the stairs and landing hard at the bottom. Very hard. Cold. Very cold.

Pain.
When would she learn?

DEREK COULD NOT GET DOWN the stairs fast enough. What was Hannah thinking, going out in an ice storm in spiky heels? To break a car window, no less! She was crazy. He'd been convinced she was bluffing or he would have made sure she stayed inside.

A dash across the foyer, the door opened, a wince at the blast of cold and the icy pellets dive-bombing his chest. At least he'd taken the time to drag on a T-shirt before he followed her. God, what a mess. He squinted out into the blizzard conditions toward her car.

Where the hell was she? "*Hannah.*"

The wind gusted, whipping her name back down his throat and reminding him in no uncertain terms that his legs and feet were bare. He stepped carefully forward and saw her. His heart jumped. She lay on her back at the bottom of the front steps—only three of them, but they were concrete. Damn it. He'd never forgive himself for not trying harder to stop her. Ignoring the cold and wet, he made it down the icy steps as quickly as possible and knelt beside her. Up close, her ragged breathing was obvious; her eyes opened in a squint; she grunted. One of the most beautiful sounds he'd ever heard.

"Hey there." He moved to shield her body from the blast and was doubly relieved when she struggled to roll up on one elbow, blinking snow from her beautiful long lashes. No major injury, to her body at least. "Did you hit your head?"

"No." She rotated her right shoulder painfully then rubbed her lower back. "Took the fall on my hip."

"Much better choice. Everything else working? Nothing broken?"

"Don't think so."

"Can you stand?" He took her wrist, helped her up, hoping she'd forget the angry words between them and let him help her. "Come inside, and I'll—"

"Oh!"

He got a sudden armful of snow-covered red-sequin-clad woman when she stumbled against him. "What is it?"

"My ankle— *Ow.*" She let loose a couple of words not allowed in either of their newspapers.

If he hadn't been so concerned, he would have rolled his eyes. Rushing out into slippery weather on shoes that no human should be able to walk in under any circumstances…just crazy. She was lucky she wasn't comatose or worse. "Is it broken?"

"I think just twisted. Maybe sprained." Her teeth chattered around her words. Her body shook.

"Come inside." He supported her into the house, thank God without resistance. In the sudden calm and blessed warmth, he kicked the door shut behind them and lowered her gently onto a chair, grabbed his black cashmere coat from the front closet, and draped it around her shivering shoulders. Then he did what he should have done the night before, punched in the code to close and lock the estate gate.

"S-stupid idea, huh."

"I've encountered better." Yet…he'd loved that same impulsive spirit in Hannah's columns. She came across as someone who danced through life trying everything that occurred to her, and while she might strike out more often than not, she also discovered places and had experiences too many other people would overlook. Or not consider possible. Or practical. Or safe.

He'd spent his whole life practical and safe. No wonder she attracted him. And astounded him. And infuriated him.

"Let me look." He took off her impractical unsafe shoes as carefully as he could. "Can you wiggle your toes? Bend your ankle? Circle it?"

"Yes. Yes. *Ow.*"

"*Ow.* Okay, let's get you upstairs. RICE for sprains, isn't it."

"R-rice?" Clutching the coat at her throat, she leaned her head against the wall, pale and drawn, snowflakes melting on her cheeks into drops he wanted to kiss dry.

"Rest, ice…something that begins with *C*…"

"Ch-champagne?"

He grinned. "Don't think so. At least not until we're sure you're okay."

"I'm okay."

"You don't look okay."

"Thanks."

"You're welcome. Let's get you into bed."

She came instantly to life, sent him a sidelong glare. "You're not g-getting me into—"

"Medical reasons, Hannah. I want you warmed up and calmed down." He slid an arm around her waist, maneuvered hers around his neck. He felt the tension in her body. "I know you're angry, but this time you can trust me."

"Only this t-time?"

He growled in frustration. "Come on."

She let him support her on the stairs to the landing, where he swept her up and carried her the rest of the way down the hall, Rhett Butler-like but with more honorable intentions. Unfortunately.

Given their recent battle, he hadn't thought he'd ever have Hannah in his arms again, which hadn't seemed such a loss until now, retroactively, when he was hit by the deep pleasure of holding her again. Wasn't he supposed to be furious still?

He didn't seem able to be when she needed him. Not to mention the genuine shock and pain on her face when he accused her of sleeping with "Jack" for a story that had undermined his confidence in her guilt. Maybe he hadn't imagined the emotion that had bloomed between them upstairs under his covers. "You'd better get out of that wet dress."

"Okay." She was shaking in earnest. He didn't stand on ceremony, set her down onto her feet, pulled the material over her head, and swept the rumpled bedcovers out of the way so she could climb carefully in, grimacing when she moved her right leg. He covered her meticulously with the sheet, then the comforter, feeling again that overwhelming sense of protectiveness, of deep satisfaction that she was with him, that he could keep her safe, help her get warm and recover.

"Better?" He crossed to his bureau to pull on a dry T-shirt, sweats and thick socks, and to escape the disturbing emotions. "I'll make you some tea."

She blinked at him. "Tea."

"You don't like tea?"

"I love tea."

"So…?"

She gave a weak but grateful smile. "Tea would be nice. I'm a little shaky. Thank you."

"Cold and shock. And you're welcome."

He went downstairs, filled the kettle that was always sitting on the stove, and put it on to heat. Maybe she'd like a couple of cookies? Rita always had shortbread somewhere, the Scottish kind made with real butter, because she knew how much he liked it. Which cabinet? And where were the tea bags?

He'd gotten too much in the habit of immersing himself in work, letting Rita and Ray take care of the house and of him, on the too-rare occasions he was here. He understood his life had been different from the average man's, but the surprise in Hannah's eyes when he could barely find the china in his own kitchen had been disconcerting and unwelcome.

He put a generous helping of the cookies he found on a plate. He and Hannah had eaten a huge meal in the wee hours, but it was near lunchtime now and, *ahem,* they'd burned quite a few calories in the interim. He glanced at the clock. Twelve-thirty. Not much sleep, and he was as full of energy as he'd been yesterday when after eight full hours he started his morning routine—exercise, shower, shave, dress, breakfast, work, work, work...

In the downstairs bathroom he found a first-aid kit he'd seen Rita taking out of the vanity. Inside, an ice pack and an Ace bandage. He added a bottle of ibuprofen to his haul and went back to the kitchen, searched for mugs and tea bags.

Mugs, he found quickly. Tea bags took longer, but he managed. At least he could make good tea, thanks to his English mother's absolute rules of how-to and how-not-to. She'd be horrified he wasn't brewing a "proper pot" with loose tea. The thought made him smile. Sometimes he did manage to smile at the memories of his mother. Too often they were too tainted with grief and bitterness at his father.

Tea bag in the mug, already rinsed with boiling water to heat it, more water poured in, he set the timer for five minutes. Even ineptly, he found he liked doing these little things for Hannah. Not that he could be glad she'd hurt herself, but...maybe she'd have time to cool off and not be in such a hurry to leave. She was right that he didn't have a leg to stand on blaming her for doing the same thing he'd done. He hadn't been completely open. But he'd have to trust her a lot more than he did now to reveal more.

He still wished she'd immediately denied having sex with

"Jack" to further her career, but a potential interview with someone like Jack Brattle might have led her over boundaries she'd not otherwise cross—and he was pretty sure she'd found more in bed with him than interview material.

Plus it was so like Hannah to jump right in at the hint of an opportunity—her blogs as well as her columns reflected that aspect of her personality. She was always first in line when new shops and restaurants opened up around the city, always immediate with her opinions and emotions. He couldn't fault her for being herself.

Or was he excusing her simply because he wanted to be closer to her than any other woman he'd ever known?

He grimaced. Men really hadn't evolved past Neander-thals. Why else would he have dragged her off to bed, knowing how complicated making love to her could turn out to be—and did turn out to be?

Complicated, yes. Yet he liked this complication. All the other complications in his life in recent years related to work. It had been a long time since his life was emotionally com-plicated, partly from not leaving himself open to anything or anyone in so long. Even now, half of him wanted to run, the other half felt on the verge of being reborn. Why now? Why her? He didn't know. And wasn't likely to figure it out any time soon. His next challenge, though, faced him immedi-ately: he needed a tray.

In a narrow cabinet next to the oven he found one, and arranged the medical supplies, tea—milk and sugar in case she wanted either—and the plate of cookies, adding a bowl of the tiny tangerines she'd liked so much at dinner and some leftover raspberries. For the final touch, he went into the greenhouse—a breath of warm, fragrant summer in the midst of a New Year's Day storm—and cut a perfect champagne rose, which he laid on the tray.

During his childhood while his parents were gone or distracted, which was too often the same thing, there had always been people—most recently and for the longest stretch Rita and Ray—kind enough to nurture him as best as they could. A flower wasn't much, but the little extra touches had made him feel someone cared enough to go to that trouble on his behalf. Though Hannah's life was probably already full of people who loved and cared for her.

The timer rang. Derek jerked out the tea bags and tossed them into the garbage, then picked up the tray. He didn't like feeling jealous, of all those people or of her. And of course the sick irony hadn't escaped him that millions of people would kill to be in his expensive shoes.

Feeling uncomfortably vulnerable, he carried his little offering up the stairs, hoping his ministrations would make her feel better. Except if she felt better, Hannah would most likely try to leave again, he hoped in a less dramatic way. Maybe it was just as well. They could put the strange and wonderful night behind them and pretend, as they'd joked, that none of it had happened. Maybe next time he was in Philadelphia he could call her, they could go out on a normal date and start over. Though with his company's Philadelphia office closing, this house selling and his leaving *The Herald*, time for trips to the city would be rare.

He reached the end of the hallway and stepped into his bedroom. One look at Hannah propped on his pillows, blond hair glistening on the dark green Egyptian cotton, her eyes sleepy, mouth soft and pink, smooth bare shoulders visible above his comforter, and he knew he had to find some way, any way—fighting fair or fighting dirty—to keep her there a whole lot longer.

6

TEA. JACK-DEREK WAS BRINGING her tea. She'd yelled at and insulted him—even if he did deserve it—what's more she'd been an impulsive idiot again and forced him outside into frigid temperatures and a raging storm in his underwear. Instead of rolling his eyes and smashing her car window to retrieve her phone himself so she could leave faster, he'd tucked her into his bed with concern and brought her tea and cookies.

And a rose. A perfect, perfect rose that smelled like summer at her aunt's house in New Jersey. No, better than that, like her high-school best friend's wedding bouquet, or like a romantic evening stroll through Society Hill's rose garden.

Aw, geez. She was still angry, her ankle hurt like hell, her shoulder and hip were bruised and stiff, she couldn't seem to get warm, yet she lost no time feeling fluttery. In her experience, men at their best made good companions and lovers, but not good nurturers. Their idea of spoiling Hannah rotten was not making her cook them dinner.

Maybe she needed to change the type of guy she dated.

"Wow." She tried to drag herself to sitting and winced.

"Easy. I brought you ice packs and an elastic bandage, too."

"Thank you." Her voice came out soft and tremulous. No, no, no, this was not the way to behave around a liar. Around liars she needed to be frosty and superior and remove herself from their company as soon as possible.

But "as soon as possible" was in a who-knew-how-long delay due to ghastly weather, said liar's lack of cooperation in handing over a phone, her car being impenetrable, her ankle having been injured... *Intrepid Reporter a Helpless Prisoner.* She sighed deeply. Helpless prisoner in a glorious mansion in the bed of a sexy handsome man who was being very, very sweet to her. Quick, someone remind her why this was horrible.

Derek laid the tray on the edge of the bed, then carefully offered her the steaming mug. "Milk? Sugar?"

"Neither. Fine straight up." She kept her eyes on the mug so she wouldn't spill and so she wouldn't betray how delighted her traitor heart was with the whole setup. Even with her brain reminding her the sexy-handsome-mansioned guy lured her here under false pretenses and slept with her without mentioning his real identity.

So? She could drink his tea and allow him to fuss over her ankle. She didn't have to fall in love with him. Again. Maybe she'd already started down that road with Jack, but she could at least be strong where Derek was concerned.

Okay? Yes, okay. As long as he'd traded in manipulator for Boy Scout, she could let him help her. After all, she was in this mess through her own clumsiness and lack of judgment, and he hadn't blinked once.

"Let's see what we can do about that ankle." He strode to the back of the room and disappeared into what must be a walk-in closet, probably the size of her entire bedroom. He reemerged carrying a thick navy bathrobe which, when placed over her chest, felt incredibly soft and smelled of Jack-Derek, which was way too pleasant for her peace of mind. She wanted to bring it home with her and take long guilty sniffs on lonely nights. Not that she was pathetic or anything. "Thanks."

"You're welcome." He slid back the covers so her body was exposed briefly to the cool air before the bathrobe came to her rescue, spread quickly over the rest of her. "Oh. Wait. I brought you ibuprofen."

He struggled briefly with the bottle, muttering, popped the top off, shook out too many pills, put two back, and presented her the others with a flourish. Then he made a face. "I forgot water."

"It's okay, I have the tea." She held up the mug and took the pills. Something about his lack of ease in certain areas contrasted appealingly with his utter confidence and suavity in others, like caring for her and food. And sex.

No, not thinking about that. Boy Scout, remember?

While he concentrated on taking the Ace bandage out of its box, she took another sip of tea, savoring the hot comforting liquid. The mug wore clusters of oversize blueberries which reminded her of pottery she'd seen at a restaurant store on a family trip to Maine. Hannah had asked for a pretty plate of this type, but her parents had been drunk and arguing, and they'd ignored her, then cruelly snapped at her when she persisted. Months later, by way of apology, a similar plate had appeared under the Christmas tree. Hannah had been pleased, but the memory of that initial unpleasantness tainted the gift. When her college roommate had broken the plate during a party, Hannah hadn't been all that upset.

"Here." Derek grabbed a burgundy throw pillow from the black mission sofa under the windows, lifted her leg, keeping her ankle straight with a hand under her heel and lowered her calf onto the pillow, while she clutched her mug and anticipated pain.

There was very little. He was very gentle.

Mmm.

"Hold there."

She sipped more tea, feeling its warmth spreading through her body, luxuriating under the softness of his robe, enjoying the feeling of being taken care of way more than a liberated twenty-first-century woman should. Tough. Let him fuss. She was due.

He wrapped her ankle a few times, molded two cleverly flexible ice packs around the swelling, wrapped those firmly in place, then removed the bathrobe and drew the lovely warm comforter back over her.

"Twenty minutes, then I'll take away the ice. You don't want frostbite on top of everything else you've been through."

"Thank you."

"You're welcome." He stood beside the bed, watching her with a slight frown.

For some bizarre reason Hannah felt suddenly and ridiculously shy. For heaven's sake, she'd been thrashing around in his bed totally naked without the slightest bit of shame all night long, now she was sensibly covered and drinking tea. What was the problem?

Maybe that she wasn't sure about the current terms of their…association. Should she ask to use his phone again? Should she yell at him some more? Apologize for her behavior? Should she—

"Cookie?" He held one in front of her mouth so she could take a bite.

"Thanks." She reluctantly took the arm not holding the mug out from under the heavenly cloud of goose down.

"Stay covered. I'll help."

"I can certainly feed myself."

"I know, I've seen you. You're very good at it." He held the cookie out insistently, then when she hesitated, brushed it across her lips, back and forth, leaving tiny crumbs she wanted to lick off. The buttery smell reached her nostrils.

Oh, she was weak. Maybe just one bite…

"Mmm."

"Good, huh. Take another one."

Another bite, the cookie crumbling marvelously between her teeth.

Another. Then she looked into his eyes, which were focused on her lips, and saw something she shouldn't have seen there. Something rather primal and possessive. And speculative. As if he were wondering what those lips of hers could be doing other than chewing a cookie.

No, no. No longer manipulator, Boy Scout. Her nurse, not her seducer. After their fight he wouldn't dare go there again.

He fed her until the cookie was gone; she felt an odd combination of satisfaction and vulnerability at being so pampered.

"Raspberry?" He held one up to her lips.

Oh gosh. She should stop this game, she felt it instinctively, but her rational brain couldn't come up with a solid enough reason. He was feeding her. She was eating. And yet… And yet… There was something more going on. "Ja— Derek, I can feed my—"

"Raspberry?"

Hannah couldn't help half a smile. Nor could she resist opening her mouth. They were talking raspberries in January. Good ones, too, fragrant and sweet. Probably had a carbon footprint the size of Sasquatch's, but as long as they were already here…

She parted her lips. He leisurely painted the ripe soft berry over them before allowing her to draw it into her mouth.

Hannah didn't look at him. Derek "Nightingale." Simply helping her get well…

"Another?"

She glanced up to find him looking a little too determinedly innocent. "I think it would be more efficient if I ate them myself."

"I'm sure it would be." He didn't offer to give the berry up.

"Um." She couldn't help a sizzle of temper. "Then, no, thanks."

"Okay." He brought the raspberry to his own mouth and against her will, she watched, trying not to get to a low point in her love life where she envied fruit. His full masculine lips parted, opened…enveloped.

Oh my. The ice and pain reliever were starting to take away the throbbing in her ankle. Her body was warming. Definitely warming. She gulped more tea. "I should go soon."

"Sure." He started peeling a tangerine.

"So…you'll let me use your cell to call out?"

"Sure." A section of the peel landed on the plate. The fresh scent rose toward her. "In a while. When you're fully recovered."

"I'm feeling fine now. Much better."

He separated a section of the orange and held it out to her. She frowned at him even while her mouth was watering.

"No?" He waved it back and forth. "Vitamin C is good for you."

Fine. It was just food. She opened her mouth, and accepted the juicy section, all business. Even so, every sense seemed to be on high alert, registering with unusual intensity the burst of pulp, the chewy membrane, the sweet tangy flavor. She wasn't going to go into what her senses were picking up about Derek. She had to get out of here before she did something stupid like beg him to make love to her again. Then she could doubly humiliate herself by falling in love with Jack Brattle and Derek Jackson on the same day.

"Tell you what."

"What?"

"Neither of us was acting completely honestly."

"True."

"So how about we clean the slate and start over?" He put the plate on the floor and held out his hand. "I'm Derek G. Jackson. Among other things I write for *The Herald.*"

She contemplated the offered hand for a second or two, then nodded and took it. At least by being friendly she'd have a better chance of using his phone and escaping to save her sanity. "Hannah O'Reilly. I write for *The Philadelphia Sentinel*, not among other things."

"Nice to meet you." His eyes were warm and brimming with mischief, which made him extremely hard to regard as merely the ticket to her exit. "Maybe you've read my Highbrow column, which helps educate Philadelphians about food worth eating."

"I might have. Once." She affected a narrow-eyed look of accusation, which didn't do anything to wipe the sexy look off his face, or to dull her reaction. "I write the Lowbrow column, which shows you don't have to be a millionaire to enjoy delicious high-quality food. Maybe you've read that one?"

"I've noticed it…"

"Hmph." Her glare became a smile in answer to his. How could she do otherwise? His grin was as contagious as a yawn.

"How did you decide to be a reporter, Hannah?"

"Oh." She waved the question into insignificance. "It was one of those childhood dreams. Other kids wanted to be actors, rock stars, firemen, I wanted to be a reporter."

He pretended to be taking notes. "And why was that?"

"Well, Doctor, in case you didn't notice, I have a passion for communicating."

"Hmm." He scribbled a few pretend words. "I did notice the passion part…"

"And why did *you* start writing, among all your 'other things.'"

"You will be shocked to learn it was a passion for communicating. The rest of my job is pretty dry. I'd written for my high-school and college paper, and it seemed like a fun and useful way to connect with people in this city, so I submitted the column idea to the *Herald* editor, Clyde Ortiz, and he went for it. Then you showed up in *The Sentinel*, people began comparing—"

"Then all my readers started reading you, and—"

"All my readers started reading you, so we both benefited." He leaned closer, focusing on her lips. "I think it's time, Hannah."

"Time?" Her voice was oddly breathless. Air wasn't going in and out of her lungs in its usual quiet way.

"To take off your ice pack."

"Oh." She didn't sound disappointed. She was sure. Not at all. Which was good because she was relieved. She'd thought he was going to use his lame apology—which now that she thought about it, hadn't even been an apology, just a plea for a truce—to seduce her again. What kind of highbrow did something lowbrow like that?

"Here." He took off the comforter, leaving her lying there again in her underwear. Only this time her modesty was not preserved with the bathrobe. He unwound the bandage, removed the ice pack and rewound the stretchy material, leaving his hand warm and strong on her shin. Nothing objectively erotic about that. Nothing. But…oh goodness. Why was the touch of a new lover so incredibly potent, where another man's hand on her shin—her shin for heaven's sake—would make her want a nap?

"Thank you."

"You're welcome." His hand traveled upward, slowly, deliberately.

She brought her good leg close, trapping the tips of his fingers just above her knees. He wouldn't. He couldn't. "What are you doing?"

"Sitting in bed with you, with my hand on your knee?"

She glared at him, fluttery all over again but determined not to show it. "Your hand is not on my knee."

"No?" He looked down in mock surprise at his fingers, which had escaped and traveled farther up her thigh.

She grabbed his hand and flung it onto the mattress. "Please cover me back up."

He shook his head, politely regretful. "I'm sorry, I can't do that."

"Why not?"

"Because I get headaches when I'm under blankets."

She gave him an are-you-crazy look. "What does that have to do with covering me up?"

"This." He put one hand on the mattress by her left hip, leaned to the right and kissed her outer thigh, lingering on her chilly skin with warm lips.

"No. Oh, no. No, you don't." She pushed at his shoulders which involuntarily jarred her leg. "Ow. You're hurting my ankle."

"No, you're hurting it." He kissed the top of her thigh, nuzzled the skin, trailed his tongue gently along the leg elastic of her panties, heading for—

"No." She tried to move away and let out a soft cry of pain.

"Don't move."

"Stop this."

"Sorry, no. Medical necessity."

"Derek."

He pressed his lips gently over the smooth fabric of her panties, unerringly landing on the small swell of her clitoris.

Fire. She was on fire. *Woman Spontaneously Bursts into*

Flames. How did this man affect her so strongly? She wanted to rip off her panties so he could plunge his tongue inside her and make her come like crazy. But she was still annoyed with him for earlier manipulation, and here he was manipulating again. If she gave in…

She'd get to come violently.

Damn it, no. That was not how she should be thinking. If she gave in, he'd get his way again, through trickery, and she'd lose every advantage of pride and probably another big chunk of her heart, too. Wasn't that always how things went with her?

"Stop. Please." She was squirming, arching, trying to figure out how to get away from him without moving her leg, trying to figure out how to get him inside her as quickly as possible. He was tearing her in half. "I don't want this."

"Your body's telling me differently."

"It has no authority to speak for me." She had to stop this. "I need to leave. *Ow.*"

Leaving was not an option. The pain was worse that time.

"Lie still, Hannah. Lie still, and it won't hurt." He deepened the pressure of his lips through her panties, biting kisses that transferred sensation and warmth where she most wanted it.

"Derek…"

"Mmm?" He slid his hand between the soft tops of her thighs, tried gently to pry her good leg away from its injured counterpart. She resisted fiercely, fists clenched, eyes screwed shut, coping with the pain in her ankle and the deep pleasure of his mouth on her.

"Open for me."

"No."

He nudged again, then his finger followed the crotch of her panties and discovered her moisture, already soaking through the material. For the first time in her life she wished for fatter thighs so he wouldn't have access between them.

"Hannah, let me in." His mouth picked up its pace along with her breathing. He found the elastic side of her panties and slid under, managed to push a finger, slowly, inevitably inside her.

She whimpered, not daring to move, but needing to desperately, so turned on she was past the point of pretending she wasn't, insistent on not letting him have his way, at the same time acknowledging the battle was all but lost. He bit gently through the red satin and lace, then rubbed in a regular rhythm with his lips, pumped inside her with his finger, and she lost control, came in a burning, overwhelming wave that drew an unfamiliar animal sound from her throat and a familiar thought from her brain.

I'm falling for you.

No. No. *No!* What had she done?

The contractions subsided. Her breathing slowed. He kissed her in a lazy line up her stomach, between her breasts and on her mouth, warm sweet kisses that made her want to wrap her arms around his shoulders and give in as she had to her desire. But she didn't want desire from his kisses or his closeness, she wanted something more, and that, for once, kept her arms at her sides.

"Angry?" He looked down quizzically, but she could sense his triumph and wasn't sure whom she was more annoyed at, him or herself.

"Not angry."

"But not happy."

"I don't know what I am. Sated, anyway."

He grinned. "Um, yes."

"That was a dirty trick. Your second dirty trick, I'd like to point out."

"Mmm, thank you."

She couldn't help laughing. "You're proud."

"But not sated."

"Well, I'm injured, so you're just going to have to suffer."

"Hmm. I don't think so." He raised himself onto his knees, removed his T-shirt, pulled down his briefs. Just the sight of his broad chest and strong thighs was enough to turn her on again, but his erection, which had made her very, very happy a couple of times already during the night, turned her on even more. Anyone would have to admit it was a thing of beauty. Not overly long, but smooth, soft and thick, the kind that let a woman know in no uncertain terms a man was inside her. In spite of her recent Richter-scale orgasm, Hannah was becoming aroused again. Especially when he met her eyes in challenge, curled his fingers around his manly thing-o'-beauty and started a graceful and experienced rhythm.

Oh, oh, oh. Everything was sexy on him. In spite of herself, she reached to help, cupping and manipulating the soft sacs of his testicles, pleased at the sharp intake of breath and speeding of his fingers that showed she had power after all.

She could do more.

Her hand trailed down his thigh, then over to her own, up to the sides of her panties. She eased them gradually down, intending to tantalize him into the same helpless lust she'd experienced.

He watched hungrily, let out a low moan.

Playtime. She let her fingers wander through her pubic curls, then drew a zigzag line up to her breasts, lifted her bra, arching to slip it off over her head. His breath came out in a rush; he said her name as if the syllables had been wrenched from his throat.

She lay back, cupped her breasts, stroked them sensually, then licked her finger and painted first one, then the other nipple with the moisture, drew another finger again between her lips, farther, in and out as if she were going down on him. His rhythm accelerated, he drew his thighs farther apart. His color was high, his lips parted, he gazed at her with feral intensity.

Hannah loved this. She'd never dreamed watching a man pleasure himself would make her feel anything but left out. But here—*she* was so clearly fueling his desire. And he was so clearly losing his mind.

Her fingers left her mouth, painted a trail down her stomach to her lower abdomen, parting her soft hair, then she slid them farther, watching his face as she slowly spread the lips of her sex open to him.

His reaction was immediate, a low hoarse sound, and the warm raining of his climax on her stomach and breasts, again and again, while his eyes locked on to hers. She felt as if the world had dwindled to this man and the intense chemistry between them.

Wasn't this supposed to feel like some kind of victory?

It didn't.

"Hannah." He rubbed his fingers through his hair, making it stand in a thick tangled mess, which made him look rumpled and sexy, and even more masculine.

A dangerous possessive sweetness spread through her heart. Oh, no. First Jack. Now Derek? She was hopeless. *Mansion Captive Becomes Prisoner of Love.*

He pulled a couple of tissues from the box on the nightstand—camouflaged by a black lacquered cover showing a flaming red dragon—and cleaned her up tenderly, then disappeared into the bathroom, returned with a warm damp washcloth and repeated the action, lingering over her breasts.

She stirred on the bed—carefully so she wouldn't hurt her ankle. The warm cloth followed by the cool air was quite, er, stimulating. So, it seemed, was anything this man did to her.

"Now." He tossed the washcloth into a wicker hamper with perfect aim and crossed his arms over his chest. "What are we going to do with you today?"

She knew what she wanted to say. But the depth of her

feeling was making her panic a little. Leaving was a good idea. Whoever came to tow poor Matilda could give her a ride home. She could ask Daphne to help if she needed anything before she made it to a doctor.

A gust of wind shook the house; ice tinkled against the windows. The thought of leaving, of the trip back in the storm, of her empty apartment, made her feel cold and lonely already. Nothing wrong with her place, it was just so…not-a-mansion-with-a-sexy-man-in-it.

She twisted her lip. Mansion? What about her refusal to worship any and all things overpriced or overwrought? Sexy man? Even though she'd given in to lust and helped generate his, she couldn't forget what he'd done to get her here.

Argh! This was all too complicated and confusing to sort out immediately and nearly impossible to do with his deep eyes and warm smile and hot bod fogging her brain.

"I should call Triple A."

"Okay." To her disappointment, he crossed to his massive dark wooden bureau without a fight and extracted a phone from one of the small top drawers.

"I wasn't kidding about not having a landline in this house." He held the cell out, too far away for her to reach it, but close enough to see that it was a BlackBerry, exactly the same model as hers. She made no move to try to grab it. "I want to make you an offer."

"Okay."

"First, I am sorry for thinking my original plan for you tonight was a good idea."

She shrugged. "I admit, it was a pretty good joke. Or it would have been…"

"If we hadn't gone animal at the sight of each other."

"Yeah, that." She couldn't stop herself from grinning.

"I'm sorry I made love to you the first time without being

clearer about who I am and what you were here for. But I'm not sorry we made love."

Hannah nodded, wishing she could sit up; lying there felt too vulnerable. She wanted desperately to accept and forget, but she couldn't decide if accepting his apology—because it really was an apology this time—would make her generous and wise, or once again a man-doormat.

"I hope you'll forgive me." His eyes were dark, sincere—he was asking, not begging. He still retained that proud quality she admired so much, yet she also got the feeling her forgiveness mattered to him. She couldn't resist that. None of it.

"You had me at *first*."

"Thank you." He chuckled, his expression warm and relieved. "Now I want to—"

"Wait." She owed him, too. Admitting the truth would strip her of her last defense, but she couldn't leave the lie out there. "I'm sorry I let you think I slept with 'Jack' only for a story. That wasn't true. I'm not like that. As soon as things, uh, heated up, I knew I wouldn't write the article. I should have admitted it right away, but I was angry. And too…proud, I guess."

"Thank you."

She had to turn away from his pleasure and the thrilling feeling that they'd crossed a line and moved closer to something wonderful. "So what's the offer?"

"Spend the day with me here. We'll start over, without the manipulation and lies, and enjoy what's left of New Year's Day together. There's plenty of food, and the roads are a mess." He tossed the phone so it lay within her reach. "If you want to, you can call and leave now. This time I won't try to stop you."

Hannah gazed at the familiar phone. So. She was free to

go. And she was free to stay. It meant a lot that he'd wanted to clear the air and that now he was letting her choose. No manipulation, no guilt trip.

She'd definitely been dating the wrong type of guy...not that this counted as dating, really. And she'd just ignore the immediate pang of longing and loss at that thought. Because that deep hunger for more of him should be enough to panic her into leaving all by itself.

Though Derek wouldn't ask her to stay unless he wanted her here, and well, it was possible for men to fall in love, too. Or so she'd heard.

She picked up the phone, registered the instant of naked disappointment on Derek's face before he dressed it with impartiality. She smiled and handed the cell back to him.

"I'd love to stay. Thank you." The flash of relief and his wide grin went straight to her heart, making her so happy she refused to listen to the voice warning her of inevitable heart-break ahead. Again.

Sometimes she thought being smart about love was the one lesson she was doomed never to learn.

7

"WAIT." HANNAH RETRACTED her arm just before Derek took back his cell phone. "I told my father I'd call him today, is that okay? He'll worry if I don't."

"Whew." He grinned, then lunged forward unexpectedly and kissed her. "I thought you wanted the phone because you'd changed your mind about staying. Absolutely call Dad. I'll be back in a few minutes."

"Okay. Thanks."

His gloriously naked body strolled out of the bedroom into the hall. Hannah clutched his phone in her fingers, little tweety-birds chirp-chirping around her head while heart-shaped fireworks exploded in the sky…and every other cliché she could think of.

Clearly she lacked a grip on reality, if not on herself. Calling Dad was a good idea for lots of reasons. Not the least of which was that she needed to remind herself that the rest of the real world and the rest of her real life still existed out there, minus truffles and pâté and a dozen bedrooms, and that whether or not she and Derek saw each other again, she'd be returning to that reality after this fantasy New Year was over.

Bummer.

She dialed hurriedly. "Dad, hi, Happy New Year."

"Hannah?" His slow voice rose uncertainly. "I didn't recognize the number. Almost didn't answer."

"I…can't get to my phone, so I'm using a friend's."

"Ah, okay."

For once she appreciated that her dad wasn't, nor had he ever been as far as she remembered, curious about her life. Anyone else she knew would jump all over the bizarre circumstance of Hannah being separated from her beloved phone. "How's Mom doing today?"

"Good. She had Cream of Wheat for breakfast. Ate it herself."

"Terrific. That is wonderful. Can I talk to her?"

"Sure." He cleared his throat, and she heard him telling her mom about the call, then extended fumbling as the receiver was handed over.

"Hannah, dear, Happy New Year."

"Same to you, Mom." Hannah's words caught in her clenched throat. She hated hearing her mother sounding so old and weak when she wasn't the former and shouldn't be the latter.

"How was the big-money party last night?"

"Big and monied. You would have hated it on both counts. I hear you're eating on your own. Congratulations."

Her mother snorted. "Yes, I'm a big girl now. Eating all by myself."

Hannah laughed, though the amusement was bittersweet. For her mother to finally confront and control her alcoholism, make it through law school, get a decent job in a prestigious firm, finally get a leg up on the family's debts, and then be reduced to pride in spooning Cream of Wheat into her own mouth… "You'll be going off to kindergarten before you know it."

"Big fun ahead, I'll tell you. In the meantime, Susie and your father are taking good care of me."

"That's great, Mom. Good for Dad. Though I know you'd do the same for him."

"I would, yes. But caretaking doesn't come naturally to most men." She paused for a slow breath. "You don't think about that when you're choosing a partner. You think you'll be young and healthy forever."

Hannah squeezed her eyes shut. Her mother's situation was so desperately unfair. "You'll keep getting better, Mom."

"That's what they say."

"Look how far you've come already."

"Yes." She sighed. "I guess I'm saying forget sex appeal when you choose a man, Hannah. It's so unimportant in the long run. Find someone who will feed you when you can't do it yourself."

Hannah instantly flashed back to the soft, sensual feel of the raspberry painted over her lips, the crumbly rough sensation of cookie. Mmm…

Oops. Not what Mom had in mind.

Another flashback to Derek carrying her into the bedroom, bringing her tea…

No. *No.* She had to stop imagining herself halfway down the aisle in her bridal white when she'd only just met someone. Worse than that, after what her mother said, with only a little effort she could imagine her and Derek fifty years from now, drinking Metamucil out of matching glasses. "I'll remember that, Mom. On my very next date I'll hand the guy a bowl of Cream of Wheat and a spoon and see how he does."

Her mom gave a rusty giggle, music to Hannah's ears. "Let me know how that works for you."

"Happy New Year, Mom. Say 'hi' to Nurse Susie."

"I will. I don't know how we'd have managed without her. You know how important work is to your father."

"Yes." Hannah managed to keep the irony out of her voice. Now that he could actually hold down a job, it was. "I do. Give him a kiss from me and sending love to you, too."

"I wish you only the best and most wonderful things this year, Hannah."

"You, too, Mom. By next New Year's Day you'll be back to taking on the legal world by storm."

"That would be very nice." She sighed again. "Goodbye, sweetie. We'll talk soon."

Hannah hung up, feeling the combination joy-sadness that wrestled in her chest these days after talking to her mom. Joy that she was alive and still her old self and sadness at the long road she still had to travel. Why couldn't the world operate perfectly all the time?

Okay, maybe that would be boring. Certainly it was unlikely. At least the troubles should be distributed more fairly. Miracle rescues aside, her parents had been through enough.

She closed the phone, then thought about calling Daphne. Her friend would have called by now and might worry when Hannah didn't return her call. Plus, Hannah wanted to check and see what was new with her boyfriend, Paul. He had been bartending when they'd met three years earlier and now worked in a bank, resisting Daphne's plan that he attend law school. Hannah wondered again if he was just rebelling against her…um, enthusiasm for ordering his life. She meant well, wanted him to fulfill his potential and all that, but…he was a grown man. All the same, Hannah would hate to see anything go wrong after three years together. Three years. Astronomically longer than any of Hannah's relationships had lasted. Maybe in the process of asking about Paul, Hannah could hint at where she was and what she was up to right now. About time she had some truly promising news where men were concerned.

An odd thump and a muttered curse made her glance toward the bedroom door. There was Derek triumphantly pushing a wheelchair. So much for Daphne. Hannah would call when she got home. At least her parents knew she was safe.

"I'd forgotten we had this chair until you needed it. Mom

used it toward the end. I'd much rather see you in it on the way to recovery."

"Derek…" His words had jolted her. "I'm sorry about your mom. When did she die?"

"Over ten years ago, and thanks." He spoke abruptly, strode over to the opposite side of the bed and dragged on the sweats and T-shirt he'd been wearing before her delicious seduction. Evidently now that he was no longer Jack Brattle, he still didn't want to share his past. Hannah tried not to feel rejected, while reminding herself wryly, again, that they weren't quite engaged yet. He didn't owe her his secrets.

But she still wanted to know them.

"Now." He returned to the wheelchair and pushed it up to the bed. "Your throne awaits. I thought you might like a guided tour of the house."

"I'd love it." She reluctantly bit off further questions—for now—and eased herself to sitting against his fabulous down pillows, clutching the comforter over her chest. Maybe he'd confide in her later. She craved more of that intimacy, to indulge more of her fantasy that he hadn't told many people the things he was telling her.

Hannah, Hannah. Always looking for signs she meant more to men than she did.

"Maybe I could borrow some clothes? Unless pushing naked women in wheelchairs is a thing for you."

He laughed and she was ridiculously happy to have put cheer back on his face.

"Fun for me, chilly for you." He crossed to his bureau and dug around in a drawer. "I looked outside. The wind has diminished, but the snow is coming down pretty hard. It's beautiful, actually. I'll show you once you're dressed."

"Just leave out the view that includes my poor car. I can't handle the carnage."

"She's got a nice blanket over her, too."

"And a tree."

"Yeah. You know, I'm not sure Triple A does trees." He shot her a mischievous look over his shoulder. "You might have to stay quite a while."

"Oh, that would be horrible." She shuddered exaggeratedly, trying her best not to grin. "With all that incredible food to finish and this big house to explore and you to…ahem, explore, too."

He opened his arms wide. "Explore me, baby."

Like she needed any more encouragement? "Okay. What do you do besides work for *The Herald?* Do you get to travel a lot? Stay in one place?"

Derek scowled. "I thought you meant ex-*plo-o-ore.* Not interrogate."

"We did ex-*plo-o-ore.* Now we interrogate."

"My luck." He rolled his eyes and tossed her a pair of sweatpants and a T-shirt like the ones he had on. "My job is to manage a family business that came to me after my parents died."

She winced. "Your dad is gone, too?"

"Yes." His face became robotic again. "He died shortly before my mom."

"Oh, no." She couldn't stand it. Ten years ago. He must have been barely out of college, if that. All that on his shoulders so young. *Man Who Has Everything Deprived of Youth.*

"But, yes, I travel. Some for pleasure as well as business. I try to mix the two whenever possible."

"I would, too, if I could." She pulled the sweatpants over her good leg, grimacing when she had to lift her bad one. In three steps he was there, helping, making her gooey inside. Making her try not to think any more about what her mother had said about snapping up caretaking men.

Travel. They were talking about travel. And she'd been back to envying his current lifestyle and all the opportunities that went with money. Sadly, no one had ever offered her all-expense-paid trips to Paris. Which they really should. "Where do you go next?"

"China. Next month." He gave her a teasing glance. "Wanna come?"

"Ooh, again?"

"I meant to China."

She rolled her eyes to douse the hot thrill and took refuge for a few seconds under the T-shirt she dragged over her head. *He was kidding, Hannah.* "Sure! I'll just cash in my checking account and let my boss know. He'll be fine."

"It's settled."

"I can do a piece on nail salons and communism and call it a business trip."

"Nail salons…"

"My boss." She lifted her hand and let it thwack his mattress on the way down. "He won't give me anything that isn't girlie. My next assignment is on women who've had boob jobs."

"Now that's a weighty topic."

She snorted. "One might say meaty."

"Ponderous."

"*Pen*dulous."

"One of the breast ideas I've heard in…I don't know."

"Recent mammary?" She mimed a quick drum-cymbal *ba-da-ba* beat. "I was thinking the lovely Dee-Dee would be a perfect subject."

"Mmm, yes."

"Mmm?" She turned on him witheringly. "Don't tell me you and she…"

"Never. I swear." He leaned forward, hands raised in

Boy Scout trust-me salute, until his mouth was an inch from hers. "Jealous?"

"No." She spoke too loudly, which plainly meant yes. All-over green with it. Though she felt a bit better when he kissed her. Okay, no, a lot better.

"You have less than no reason to be. Let's get you ready to roll." He helped her on with a much-too-big pair of thick gray cotton socks. "And I want to hear more about what you want to write. Though I can't imagine anything more satisfying than breasts."

She let him know with her eyes exactly what she thought of that comment. "Obviously I want to write about more substantive things."

He paused, leaving his hand on her good ankle, good humor dissolving into a frown aimed down at the loose floppy sock. "Like...Jack Brattle?"

"Oh. Well, yeah." She sighed wistfully. "That would have been a dream come true. After a scoop like that, I could have had the clout to write about... Well, never mind."

"About what?"

"About anything."

"Hey." He raised his eyebrows expectantly. "This is my interrogation. Answer the question."

"Yes, *sir*." She saluted, pleased he really wanted to know. "I found out this drug, Penzyne, used for treating depression, has shown promising results as a treatment for diabetes. However, it's ten times cheaper than the drugs sold now, and the company doesn't want to decrease their profit margin. Seems to me that's important information a lot of suffering people should know."

He put his hands on his hips, staring with a perplexed look on his face, until she started to feel as if she should tell a joke to break the tension. "It was...selfish of me to play the Highbrow trick, Hannah. I was thinking of the one-up-on-you score, not of what pulling Jack out from under you would represent to your life and career. Or how it would feel. I'm sorry."

Whoa. She had to look away from his sincerity. Instinct told her he didn't make apologies a habit, that this had been a rare and painful event. The fact that he'd done it for her…

Well, gee whiz, she should tell him her ring size and be done with it.

"Thank you, Derek. It's okay. The joke would have been great if it hadn't gotten…" She gestured aimlessly.

"Complicated."

"That's one way of putting it." Very complicated. More than he knew.

"You ready?"

"For anything." She let him lift her into the chair, though she probably could have managed on her own. But who could resist the chance to feel the power in those arms and shoulders and to be held, all too briefly this time, against that magnificent chest?

Clearly not her.

"Let's go." He turned her chair, then paused. She peeked back and caught him putting a couple of condoms into the pockets of his sweatpants.

"Excuse me, what kind of tour is this going to be?"

"I hope a really, really fun one."

She laughed as he maneuvered her out of the bedroom and pushed her down the hall. She was eager for the tour, not only because she was interested in finding out more about the house and exploring it leisurely, but also because this would be her first normal time with Derek, time when they weren't either feasting, flirting, fighting or—

That other *f* thing. Though maybe those condoms would come in handy…

"Now, this…" He stopped outside the first door on the left,

which gave onto an attractive masculine room done in royal-blue and hunter-green. "This bedroom is where my uncle Chris grew up. You can find dirty words and limericks carved on the inside of the closet door. He used to hide in there for hours."

"Wow. Go, Chris." She loved it. *Black Sheep in the Jackson Pasture.*

He rolled her farther down the hall and to the right, by another bedroom in muted crimson and powder-blue with pale pink sprigged wallpaper.

"This one belonged to my Aunt Sue. Knocked up at seventeen. My very conservative grandfather disinherited her. No one knows where she is now."

"Ouch. Poor girl." An even blacker sheep. Obviously Hannah had assumed people with so much money lived charmed lives. Ridiculous now she thought about it. Life happened to everyone. Though she still maintained the bad times would hurt less if you could pay for anything you needed.

"And this one." He pushed open the door to reveal an absolutely minuscule room, which meant it was practically the size of hers. Most likely meant to be a closet, it had a bed-sized mat on the floor, a set of bare metal shelves and a wooden bench. Period. "This was Uncle Frank's room. Weird kid. Grew up to be a weird adult."

"Why doesn't that surprise me?" She examined the unusual furnishings, wondering why they hadn't been changed. "Is anyone apple-pie normal in this family?"

"Nope," he said cheerfully.

"You, anyway."

"Don't be too sure."

"Which was your room?"

"Ahh." He pushed the chair down the hall and opened a large door to the left of the stairs.

Hannah gaped. "You have an *elevator* in your house?"

"What, not everyone does?"

She rolled her eyes and let him push her on. "Oh. Yeah. Um, I guess ours was always being fixed."

"See?" He grinned at her expression and rotated a lever on a dial set into the wall toward the number three. "My great-grandfather had terrible arthritis, so he had this installed. And look, it's coming in handy."

"True enough." She listened to the appealing rattle-clank of the ancient machinery and hoped it had been inspected fairly recently. "I guess money goes back generations in your family."

"You don't think I earned all this as a newspaper man?"

She snorted. "Trust me, that never occurred to me."

"Well, Hannah, the ugly truth is that the family has never lacked for cash. Great-great-grandfather made the fortune."

"In what?"

"Here we are." He slid back the gate and opened the door onto the third floor.

Hannah stared, openmouthed, trying to process what she was seeing. "Oh my gosh."

"Thought you'd like it."

She wasn't sure she had moved to *like*. She was still stuck on *flabbergasted*. "*This* was your *room?*"

"Yes."

Would she ever be able to take this in? Rooms opened one into another, so the effect was of one continuous space—make that an entire mansion floor of continuous space. To the left, a normal bedroom area, or rather a normal rich kid's bedroom area, in navy and white, with a beautiful sleigh bed, matching dresser and table, a multilevel desk and a smart navy and white rug covering the hardwood. Branching off from there, the "bedroom" left off, and the fantasy began.

A large central area directly off the elevator had a jukebox, soda and snack vending machines along one wall, and a glossy wooden dance floor, ready for action. In the next room she could see the corner of a Ping-Pong table and most of a small trampoline. After that, a mini-movie house with rows of theater-style seats and a popcorn maker. The place should be in Wikipedia to define *overindulged.*

But wait! There was more…

Derek rolled her forward past a wall of stereo equipment and floor-to-ceiling shelves of CDs; a room with a stage, a puppet theater and racks and boxes of costumes; a room with gymnastic equipment and mats, security harness dangling from a complicated track on the ceiling; a music room with piano, guitars, drums and karaoke machine. An elaborate setup in the next, with electric trains that ran around mountain and valley landscaping and several villages with assorted vehicles and tiny figures. A room with tables, easels, art supplies and a whole wall of board games. Finally a library with half-a-dozen long, four-tier bookcases bursting with books, a computer, a study carrel and chairs and table arranged around a fireplace.

She was exhausted just looking. Nothing prepared her to equate what she'd just seen with the words *my room.* And yet for all its splendor, it had an abandoned quality, as if it had spent too many years as a sad museum instead of the play space it should be.

"I spent a lot of time in this library." He parked her by the fireplace and crossed to one of the shelves, running his large strong hands over what were doubtless familiar titles. "I was kind of a nerd, I guess."

"You didn't have brothers or sisters?" She bet she already knew the answer. She was just trying to wrap her mind around one person having all this, when there were so many kids for whom any one piece would be a fantasy so far out of reach, they could dream about it for an entire childhood. Like her, about two decades ago. Heck, her now.

"Nope." He dropped into one of the armchairs and thoughtfully traced an ink stain on the upholstery, maybe remembering how it got there. "I'm sure it looks…extreme for one boy."

"Yuh." He had no idea. Her big-thrill toy was a set of chipped metal doll furniture that had been her grandmother's.

Derek sat back in the chair, watching her too closely, probably sensing her discomfort. Then he leaned forward, resting his elbows on his thighs, and her greedy body lost no time feeling the hum of sexual electricity at his nearness. "It's too much. I know. My parents…they thought if they gave me enough toys it wouldn't matter that they had no interest in being parents."

Hannah nodded. She knew what it felt like to have parents too distracted to parent. But…he had *this*. My God. "You must have had friends over constantly."

"Occasionally. I was a loner. And we didn't live here that often."

A loner. Surrounded by a kid paradise. And they didn't live there often? Why not? What did that mean? "So all this just sits here?"

"Yeah." Her question obviously puzzled him. "Why, you want to play with me?"

"I'm not really in shape for gymnastics at the moment."

"You managed fine downstairs." He grinned, and she blushed idiotically. "The truth is, I don't spend much time at this house, and I'm constantly busy with…" He tightened his lips. "Things that don't matter to me very much."

She couldn't understand that. "*I* know what that feels like. But with your money you'd have to be free to do whatever you want."

"You'd think so."

But…

The word stayed unspoken. Obviously the little people like her didn't understand his world. She wouldn't pretend to.

"I'm selling the house."

Hannah jerked her head back to him, instantly dismayed. She didn't expect that. At all. The revelations about his great-grandfather, his batty uncles and wayward aunt had made her feel the house was steeped in Jackson tradition and always would be.

"You're moving."

"We're closing our Philadelphia office, so I—"

"Where are you moving to?" How could he? She'd just found him. And he was *leaving?* The dating gods had gotten her once again. What a joke. Ha ha ha.

"I don't really live anywhere, Hannah. My parents were restless. When the family troubles hit, they found moving around honored their privacy more than staying in one place. And they wanted this original family house protected as much as possible from the media. I was mostly alone here, in the charge of the property caretakers." He glanced around moodily. "I guess I inherited Mom and Dad's taste for roaming."

But…he'd still be visiting, wouldn't he? "Why sell?"

"Now the office is closing I have no reason to return."

All her strength was needed not to look as if she'd been sucker punched. "Well, but…it's your home."

"I don't have great memories of my childhood. My parents and I weren't exactly best friends."

"I didn't have that, either."

He looked surprised. "You seem so close to them."

"Uh…" Her turn to look surprised. How would he know? "I do?"

"After your mom's stroke and your dad's orchestra nearly going under...you sounded deeply concerned."

"How did you..." She stared at him, mind spinning furiously. The newspaper world was small, but not that small. How could—

Her mental lightbulb switched on. "You read my blog."

He nodded. "Frequently over the past year."

"Really." She was astonished...then pleased. Then *thrilled.* If he'd read her blog, that meant—

"I enjoy it a lot. Another reason I wanted to meet you." He gave a crooked smile. "Though I went about it in a pretty underhanded way."

"You should have shown up at *The Sentinel* and jumped me."

"I wish I had."

She laughed automatically, her mind processing the new information, trying in her typical way to make it point toward something that would bring them together. He'd been reading her blog. He wanted to meet her. He hadn't just been out to trick her, then been overcome by lust on the spur of the moment. He'd actually admired, liked, been curious about her before tonight—or, well, make that yesterday night.

Steady, Hannah. That didn't mean he'd fallen for her or that he was going to. But...it sure beat unreasoning lust on sight. And with the way he'd looked at her, handled her as if she was the most precious gift he'd ever been given... *Hope Springs Eternal in Oft-Trampled Heart. "I Can't Help Myself," Woman Says.*

"I'm...glad things are better for your mom and dad." He cleared his throat, looking self-conscious.

"Thanks. It was miraculous that they got help when they needed it."

"Life is messed up no matter what your circumstances." He got to his feet, but she pushed the wheelchair back before he could walk past her.

"Hold on, we need to change that attitude."

Derek's eyebrows rose. "We do?"

"Oh." She felt herself blushing. *Nice going, Hannah.* Every man's worst nightmare: a woman who'd try to change him. She hadn't really meant it that way. She just…aw, hell, she just wanted him to be happy. "No, I mean—"

"I know what you mean, Hannah." He bent and kissed her, causing electric crackles that soothed to sweetness when he stroked her hair back from her face. "I'm afraid my problems go deeper than the time we'll have together to solve them."

Ouch. She hadn't wanted to hear before, but there it was. Of course. They'd just met, had a lovely promising beginning and, oh, look, here came The End. Story of Hannah's life. Not for her the series of normal pleasant dates everyone else expected and got, followed by a natural commitment to an exclusive relationship and an investment in hope for a future together.

No. She dove straight in—to arms, to bed, to love, lured by the promise of The One, Her Soul Mate. And always she found out she was wrong.

But this was worse. Because beyond the usual attraction, and I-can't-wait sexual drive, she saw how he needed her and how he could make her happy. And she saw how their differences could complement and teach each other, instead of driving them apart. Enough there to be worth exploring. More than enough.

He'd said he had no reason to return. But…

Sparks of determination lit a corner of her gloom. It was a long shot. A very long one. Maybe, though, over the next hours, days, or weeks, whatever time they still had together, she could convince Derek Jackson he had the very best reason of all.

Her.

8

Derek rolled Hannah back into the elevator, closed the gates and turned the control lever to the first floor. Seeing his childhood room through her eyes had been an educational experience. He was so used to the awed and envious reactions of the few friends he'd shown it to—mostly kids in grade school—that he was unprepared for how an adult stranger would judge it. And him.

So much of his childhood he'd spent alone that he felt he'd been anything but spoiled. Sure, he had a lot of toys. A lot of cool stuff. But the toys his parents bought never came close to giving him what he needed from them.

Now, however, he saw the room as something new. A waste, for one. Her disapproval had made him want to redeem himself. Ha! Since when did other people's opinions of him count? His parents had disdain for nearly everyone. And here he was, the apple close to a tree he'd wanted to chop down for as long as he could remember.

The elevator stopped. He pulled the gate, pushed open the door and wheeled Hannah through, his enthusiasm for the tour dampened. She wouldn't enjoy the lavish ballroom, the formal dining room, the pool, or indoor tennis court, either. Why had he thought they'd impress her? Because they did most people? He should have figured out by now that Hannah was anything but "most people."

"Where next, Captain?"

However… "Would you like to see the greenhouse?"

"I'd love to. Unless it's full of snow and icy steps."

"Neither. I promise." He guided her down the hall past the kitchen, the second parlor and to the left to bring them to the back of the house. Ahead, the door to the greenhouse promised warmth and greenery. This he knew she'd like.

"Here we are." He opened the door and rolled her in, felt a wave of satisfaction when she gave an exclamation that showed, yes, she thought this, at least, was money well-spent. He had to agree.

Rita handled the household duties, and Ray, a green-thumbed genius workaholic, tackled the handyman jobs and the grounds. The greenhouse was and always had been his pride and joy. Derek's mother had loved flowers, especially orchids and roses, and had given him carte blanche in selecting and maintaining whatever he thought would please her. Which was too often whatever she thought other people wouldn't have and would envy.

"Who takes care of all this?" Hannah breathed in the humidity and floral scents rapturously. "I'd spend my whole day here if I were you."

"You like to garden?"

"I'm sure I would if I had one. I tried to grow a few flowers indoors, but I don't get enough light in my apartment, and they all died eventually. I tried again outdoors, but someone stole the pots off the fire escape, and that was that."

He frowned, not liking the idea of her cooped up in a tiny dark home. Nor did he like the idea of her being around thieves, even just plant thieves. "Ray takes care of the greenhouse. He and Rita manage the estate."

"What will they do when you move?"

He smiled wryly. Did she think he'd kick lifelong staff—

and friends—out into the cold when he no longer had use for them? He'd be disturbed by her accepting the cliché of cold-hearted wealth, except too often his family embodied it.

"They were provided for in my parents' wills. They're planning to retire to Oregon." He gestured to the snow, still coming down hard. "Ray wants a longer growing season."

"Don't blame him."

He pushed her forward amid the greenery, seedlings in pots on small tables of varying heights and areas landscaped by Ray's gifted eye for color, texture and composition. Derek found himself talking about the plants, pointing out the rare ones, showing her how Ray had molded and tended others, how he'd grouped them according to countries and regions of origin. He was surprised how much he remembered from those days when he'd tagged along behind Ray as he made his rounds, watering, pruning, sensing what each plant needed in a way Derek could never hope to intuit.

"Oh, roses." Hannah clapped her hands. They'd stopped at his mother's favorite spot, a small stone bench surrounded by various fragrant and colorful species. "This must be where you got the one for my tray. They're exquisite. I could spend the next several hours just smelling them."

"And so you shall." He strode to the back wall of the green-house, to the neatly organized storage area that held Ray's tools, and retrieved the pruning shears, filled an etched crystal vase with tepid water to immerse the stems in. The way he felt right now—like Christmas morning did to children—he wouldn't rest until he'd cut every rose in the whole place and presented them to her. Somehow making her happy had become the same thing as making himself happy.

His hand stilled on the vase handle. Unless he was wrong he was well on his way to falling unexpectedly and irration-ally in love with Hannah. He'd probably been halfway there when he'd arranged to lure her to the estate in the first place. His obsession with her blog and columns wasn't only due to his admiration for her writing skills and her intimate knowledge and love of the city. He hadn't hired a nurse for her mother and bailed out her father's orchestra because he was noble. Something about her had inspired him, attracted him, gotten to him deeply from the very start, had him acting in ways he'd never acted before. New acts, new thoughts, new feelings…new Derek.

Even the thought of the word *love* made him what another man might consider giddy but on him felt finally and completely alive. Maybe Hannah was sent by a guardian angel to kick his lame ass back into the land of the living.

Fanciful, but that's the kind of mood he was in, very uncharacteristic. Too many happenings during this night had been magical for it to seem like a normal series of events. Though there was one other possible explanation, which would probably never have occurred to his old self. Maybe *he'd* been sent by *her* guardian angel, to help make her life into more of what it should be. To help her family, yes, but money wasn't the only thing she needed. He had the means to provide exactly what she wanted, to take her where she wanted to be.

He could get her the interview with Jack Brattle.

Back at her side, he perused the roses, hardly seeing them. It would be tough to have Jack's story out there for the world to read, when Mr. Brattle had kept himself and his life so private for so long. Derek wasn't sure he'd be willing to make that sacrifice, even for a journalist as worthy as Hannah.

"Derek?"

He blinked and realized he'd gone frozen staring at the roses with shears raised in his hand, probably looking as if he were posing for a horror movie poster. "Sorry. What colors do you like?"

"I'd hate for you to cut them." She shook her head at the array of bushes, her eyes glowing with wistful pleasure. "They're so beautiful here."

"They'll be more beautiful in your home, with you." He didn't like thinking of her going back there. He didn't like thinking of her going anywhere. Maybe it could snow for the rest of her life.

Safety catch released, pruners ready, he started cutting, laying the blooms in her lap as he went. White, burgundy, pink in two shades, yellow, lavender, red, peach—

"Derek, stop." Her protest was made while laughing. "There won't be any left."

He knelt in front of her, picked up a rose, holding her gaze so she'd really listen and really understand each one was selected for her. "Pink for grace."

Her laughter stilled. She watched him put the stem into the vase of warm water, suddenly shy.

"White...for youthfulness and humility."

"Hmph." Her show of petulance didn't completely hide her pleasure. "I notice you didn't say purity or innocence."

"*And*—" he glared in mock reproach "—white also stands for silence."

A giggle transformed her faux pout. "Shutting up. Go on."

"Burgundy." He drew the velvet bud down her face. "For unconscious beauty."

A blush started where the rose had traveled, as if it had transferred its beautiful color to her cheek.

"Peach for sincerity. Pale pink for joy." He arranged the blooms carefully beside the others in the vase and selected the next, praying she didn't think he was a total sap. He wasn't so sure he wasn't one. Her fault entirely.

"Yellow..." He smiled into her eyes. "For the promise of a new beginning."

Her breath went in; her gaze dropped to her hands. He was pretty sure she didn't think he was a sap.

"Red for courage and passion." His voice had lowered, become thicker. He set the red rose in the vase, almost completing the riot of color he wanted. One more.

"Lavender." Nearly whispering now, he rested the perfect bloom against her perfect lips. "Lavender for love at first sight."

She didn't move, didn't even raise her eyes. He held his breath. If she laughed or worse, withdrew politely, he'd want to lock his life away again, forever.

Then a tear slid slowly down her left cheek, and his heart melted. He dropped the flower in her lap, took her shoulders and kissed her with everything he felt in his heart.

She responded tentatively, then her arms crept around his shoulders, and her mouth softened, opened, her tongue swept his, and passion erupted. He drew back, ran his hands down her sides, drawing his thumbs deliberately over her breasts. Her breath caught; her body arched into his touch. At her hips he stopped, eased her to the front edge of the wheelchair seat.

"Will it hurt if I lift you?"

"Tour's over?" She blinked in innocent mischief.

"No, we're just getting to the climax."

She laughed, drew his head down as if for a kiss, then surprised him by painting his lips, slowly and sensually with her tongue. His cock hardened further. He lifted her as gently as he could, heard her quick inhale signifying pain.

"I'm sorry."

"I'm fine." She wrapped her arms around his neck, wrapped her good leg around his back. He walked slowly, careful not to bang her foot, and settled her onto Ray's potting table, kept meticulously clean as usual.

Hmm. He'd never thought about the table being the ideal height for sex, but now he'd never see it any other way.

"Derek."

"Yes." He stepped between her legs, moved her thick hair to one side and tasted the soft pale skin of her neck.

"Are you…did you mean…" Her voice trembled. "The lavender rose…"

He kept her face next to his, sure vulnerability would over-whelm him if he met her eyes. "Did you feel it?"

"Yes." She kissed his throat, his chin, finally hovered a fraction of an inch from his mouth. "I did."

He moved that fraction of an inch and met her lips again, felt his brain turn to pudding. Nothing he'd experienced with a woman had ever approached this tornado of want and need and fear and joy.

Being a guy, however, he knew what he wanted next, how to show her what he felt without having to resort to more words or more flowers. And frankly, the sight of her breasts against the material of his T-shirt was liquifying his pudding-brains further.

She was attractive, intelligent, talented, he respected her, yes—but, oh man, she was also one of the hottest women he'd ever met.

The T-shirt had to go first. It surrendered easily as he pulled it up and over her head, leaving her breasts bare, open to him, for him. He palmed them greedily, taking one, then the other into his mouth, tuning in to her moans and gasps of pleasure.

The snow might end—it was slowing already—she might leave the house, but she wasn't leaving his life. Not any time soon. Not until they both found a damn good reason they wouldn't suit—or until one of them died of old age.

Her hands tugged at his shirt, and he obliged her by taking it off, letting out moans of his own as her teeth and lips closed over his nipple and her hands slid down into his sweats, cupping his buttocks, bringing his erection closer to where it wanted to be.

Their kisses turned hot, eager, tinged with desperation. He loved her. He wanted her. He needed to be inside her so badly he was ready to scream.

She swayed side to side, edging her sweatpants over her hips, letting them fall. He knelt and eased the elastic cuffs over the ridiculously large socks he'd loaned her—a look he'd find incredibly sexy from now on—kissed his way up her bare smooth legs, pausing to bury his face between them, to arouse her, and to sate his need to taste. But this wasn't how he wanted her to come. He wanted her to come while they were face-to-face, so he could experience her climax with her, make sure she knew he was the one bringing her the ecstasy.

He stood, dug a condom out of the pocket of his sweats before he pushed them down around his ankles. He'd take it slow, stimulate her carefully to make up for the lack of foreplay, but he wanted and needed that more intimate connection now.

The condom went on swiftly. He stood watching her for a few long seconds, memorizing her face as if this was the last time they'd be together. He knew it wasn't. But he wanted to remember this moment forever, the first time he'd made love to a woman he cared for more than anything else he'd ever cared for. His life felt new, and he intended Hannah to be part of it.

All this in less than twenty-four hours.

"Hi." He grinned at her, pretty sure he hadn't felt this happy in…ever.

"Hi." The way her face glowed made him dare to think she felt the same way. Was there anything better than this?

Yes.

He moved close, caught her upper lip, then her lower between his, leisurely biting kisses that made her whimper. "Something you want?"

"You."

He put his forehead against hers, stroked her cheek. "You've got me, Hannah."

"I want nothing less." Her fingers traveled through his hair, down his back; she smiled suggestively. "But I also want something more."

"It's yours." He guided his erection against her, concentrating on every sensation, then pushed deeper with each gentle thrust. She was tight—he hadn't spent enough time. "Am I hurting you?"

"Mmm, no. No." She wrapped her arms around his back, urged him on.

He pulled back, moved forward slightly farther, pulled back and did it again, making sure he wasn't forcing, making sure his erection glided gently where it belonged, inch by slow inch.

One final pull back, another long thrust that made her groan in pleasure, and he was in to the hilt and could relax and start his rhythm. In and out. The scents of the greenhouse surrounded them; humidity made sweat dew their bodies. In and out. In and out. Outside them, everything was cold and white and severe; around them only green and warmth and life; between them heat and passion.

In and out, he made love to her, catching her chin sometimes to gaze into her eyes, seeing his feelings and his arousal reflected there. In and out, hands spreading her legs wider, leaning back so they could both look down and watch the beauty of what they were doing.

In and out, thumb to her clitoris, bringing her to the brink then letting her down again.

In and out. Nothing in his life had ever been as precious as this moment, the two of them together, stranded in the cocoon of a summer paradise.

This was the one thing he had never been able to find. The

one thing his money couldn't buy. The one thing he'd been hungering for, the thing that had drawn him to Hannah, and the reason he'd pursued her. Her vitality. Her joy. A chance to relive his lost youth as he approached the middle of his life.

In and out. He gathered her closer, murmured words into her hair, sweet tender words he wouldn't have thought himself capable of. Always in and out, stroking her, and with the movement stroking himself as nature intended.

"Derek?"

"Yes." He drew light circular designs down her back.

"I…don't— I've never…" She made a sound of frustration. "I don't know how to say this."

"You don't have to say anything."

"It's…this is so amazing," she whispered. "Don't move away. Don't leave."

He wanted to say he wouldn't. He wanted to reassure her, but in the middle of this overwhelming sensual and emotional experience, wasn't a good time to rethink a major life decision.

"Hannah…"

"It's okay. You don't have to answer. I… It was the only way I could think of to tell you how this feels."

He only had one way to respond. He kissed her, over and over, accelerating his rhythm until he started breathing in short bursts. He felt his pleasure rising to where it would soon be out of hand.

Hannah. He drew his body back just far enough to slip a finger between them. In less than a minute he had her slippery and writhing around his cock.

"Oh." She gasped; her nails dug into his shoulders. Her body flushed, and he knew she was close. *"Oh."*

He took his finger away, dug his hands under her beautiful firm hips and plunged harder. He felt her coming a second before he lost his own control.

Hannah.

He stayed inside her for a long time, holding her, not wanting to break the connection either physically or emotionally, not wanting to return to reality, to the tough and complicated decisions ahead, half-afraid that once the spell of her presence was removed, the decisions would be made for him, like most of the decisions in his life. That when given the chance to ditch his past and start out new, the tentacles of habit and duty would clutch at him, and he'd be unable to break free.

Now, though, wasn't the time to think about that. Now was the time to think about Hannah's soft skin and eager lips, her beautiful body and her gift for bringing happiness, the dozens of ways he wanted to bring happiness back to her.

Like giving her Jack Brattle.

He opened his mouth to offer the interview…and couldn't. Not now. Not yet. In a moment like this, he didn't want to introduce a man who had something Derek Jackson couldn't give her. Not for the first time, and only for a few useless bitter seconds, he hated Jack Brattle and everything he stood for.

Because giving Jack to Hannah meant losing part of himself.

9

THERE WAS NO DOUBT NOW. None. Hannah was in love. Again. Only more. As far as she was concerned all the other men had been warm-ups, appetizers, *amuse-bouches*. With Derek she felt ten times the passion, ten times the respect, ten times the enjoyment, ten times the surety.

He was The One. *Woman Finds True Love in Hothouse Sexfest.*

"Going up." He pushed her wheelchair onto the elevator and turned the control lever to take her back upstairs.

Yes, she knew she thought one or two other guys might have been The One before him, but, no, really, that had only been briefly, say after two dates and sex once or maybe twice. She and Derek had been together all night and nearly an entire day, which counted as three or four dates at least, and they'd had sex many times. Yes? Yes. See?

Maybe under twenty-four hours seemed too quick, even for her, but Derek was quality over quantity. Besides, everyone said you just knew when you met the right man, and she did. *This* time for real.

Really.

Not only that, but he felt the same way. He must. Because he'd given her the lavender rose and whispered, "Love at first sight." For once she wasn't the only one struck by an instant thunderbolt. For once Eros had aimed arrows at the man, as well. Took him long enough. Little bastard.

But then, she shouldn't be too hard on him. Maybe the demigod had a plan all along. To drag her through the dating dregs so that when she met Derek she'd be sure he was right, having had so many wrong experiences, and so that he'd be more than worth the wait.

"Second floor. Everybody out." He opened the gate and door and wheeled her into the hall.

Bliss! Perfection!

Well, near-perfection. When she stopped to think about it, the whole "I'm Jack Brattle" deception still stung, but not like a thorn, more like a grain of sand she'd turn into a pearl. And of course, in her typical fashion she was coping by trying not to think about it. Denial could be a very good and useful friend. Besides, that incident had happened wa-a-ay back then. Yesterday. Before she and Derek had started to trust each other, before they'd gotten this close.

Hannah blew out a breath that made her bangs sail outward. All that sounded so lovely and felt so right and so true. So why were her inner demons starting a cynical chant in her head?

She fought to shut them out. No, she wasn't just being stupid again. This time she wasn't. This time…

Well…she trusted this man more than she trusted herself.

"Now arriving. Bedroom on track four."

In the greenhouse after they'd made love in every sense of the phrase, she'd leaned against him for a long time, feeling his heart thumping under her cheek, his arms holding her securely, breathing in the wonderful fragrances around them. Oh la la, could someone please invent a moment-preserver? Because that particular moment didn't deserve to happen once and be lost forever.

Hannah had wanted time to stop, didn't want anything about her life or their relationship—and oh, how sweet to use that word without fear—to get more complicated or less beautiful than it was right then.

Silly, she knew, unreal for sure, because no relationship could grow and bloom without its share of troubles, but that was what she'd wanted. Minutes had ticked by with neither of them moving. Finally, a load of snow had rumbled off the roof and thudded onto the yard, startling them both, breaking the spell, leading them to smiles, kisses and, since they'd both agreed to shower before dinner, up here to the—

"Bathroom. Last stop."

Oh my lord.

By now she would have been shocked and probably disappointed if his bathroom—or what had been his parents' bathroom—was anything but amazing. The room was enormous of course, tiled in elegant gray and cream. Rich mahogany cabinets. Muted wallpaper with a tiny gray pattern. Cream towels about twice the size and thickness of hers, hanging on what looked like an electric warming rack near the shower door. Brass faucets, cream sink and toilet, thick gray rugs, and the whole effect brightened by a fresh green air fern growing from a brass pot on a small glass table near the sink.

Then…the shower, which was the size of her entire bathroom for starters, made of slightly frosted glass that echoed the gray in the rest of the room.

"Gee." She looked around as if she were deeply disappointed. "I expected it to be fancy."

"Yeah, Mom and Dad were noted for their frugality." He stepped around the chair, helped her up and out of her clothes, the perfect gentleman except for a tendency for his talented, lovely hands to linger affectionately on her naked skin, which she found, coming from this gentleman, not at all objectionable. And in fact, she herself was ladylike enough to keep from jumping his body as it emerged from its clothes, but when he bent to take off his socks, she felt it extremely necessary to trail her palm over the smooth solid platform of his back.

"We're ready." He put an arm around her, supporting her as she limped toward the shower door. "I know the third floor overkill was more shock than pleasure, but you liked the greenhouse, and—"

"I *loved* the greenhouse. Especially your table manners."

"Mm, yes." He kissed her temple. "I think you are going to enjoy this, too."

Oh, yes, she was. Inside the stall, a bench where she could sit comfortably, and on the walls, the ceiling—everywhere it seemed—about a dozen showerheads, wide ones. When he turned them all on, she insisted on standing, stretching out her arms, lifting her face. It was like being caught in a glorious spring deluge, the kind that is so warm and inviting you don't care if your clothes get wet. Only they weren't wearing any, which was even better.

She could get used to this. And to the way they leisurely soaped and shampooed each other, hands always in motion over slick skin. At every touch of his fingers, she expected their chemistry to kick in, but it never did. Instead, she fell into a quiet sensual contentment more satisfying than if they'd gone at it again in the shower. Which, mmm, maybe sometime they'd get to. But together like this, they weren't doing, or wanting, or needing anything from each other, they were just being. It felt so right, she couldn't fathom that twenty-four hours earlier they hadn't even met. She'd almost believe in past-life existences if they explained the degree to which she felt she'd always known him.

They rinsed off for far too long, given that water, especially water pouring down in such delicious torrents, shouldn't be squandered. But even though she believed firmly in conservation and took quick no-nonsense showers at home—where one showerhead seemed plenty, *ahem*—here amidst all this luxury she felt there couldn't possibly be a shortage of anything anywhere. As if the planet's rules applied to other people who lived in the real sad world, not here. Maybe that was part of his heritage, part of the entitlement he'd grown up with. Maybe that was why the room upstairs had been left undisturbed. Because in his mind, it was just his room, to preserve or destroy as he wanted.

"Having fun?" He grinned down at her, water droplets on his cheeks, dripping from the ends of his hair, running in streams down his chest and arms.

Her heart started to swell and then bypassed love into unexpectedly deep vulnerability tinged with panic. What if he really did move away? What if his flower speech in the greenhouse was a rehearsed routine? Or the opposite, a whim of the moment, Derek carried away by the circumstances? What if he woke up after she went home and thought, *Hmm, good lay, time to move on…*?

He might. Men did. Especially with her. *She* wouldn't, she knew that. She'd carry some part of this man with her until the day she died.

"Had enough? Your ankle bothering you?" He put steadying hands around her waist, moved her closer to help support her weight. He must have mistaken the fear on her face for pain.

"No, I'm okay." She clung to him, savoring the warm hard length of his body braced against hers. "I was thinking I need a shower like this in my apartment. Maybe if I took out the living room it would fit."

He reached and turned off the water, grabbed a towel from

outside the stall, and wrapped it around her shoulders. Yes, she'd been right about the warming rack.

"Does my money bother you?"

"No. Of course not." Her denial came out too quickly.

"Really."

Hannah sighed. *Tell the truth.* They were all about truth now. "It's…not what I'm used to. It's not who you are, either."

"Not totally." He was watching her intently. "But it is part of me."

"And abject poverty is part of me." She grinned and used a corner of the towel to dry a drip traveling down his forehead. "Though not so much anymore."

"The cliché is true, Hannah, there's more to life than money." He grabbed the edges of her towel and drew her close, grinning mischievously, then bent his head toward her. "For example, there's this…"

Oh, yes, there was, and thank goodness. She could happily be kissed by him for the rest of the day. She wouldn't need food, sleep, nothing…the kissing equivalent of his air fern.

When he drew back, she could barely remember what they'd been discussing except that it had been serious. Not as serious as how gorgeous he looked with his eyes alight, hair in wet curls, cheek rough with masculine stubble.

"You know, you never told me how your family made its fortune."

"I didn't, no." He turned away and grabbed a towel for himself, draped it around his hips. "I also didn't tell you, which I've been meaning to, that I've been to every restaurant and shop you've recommended since I started reading your column last summer."

She was so astonished she let him get away with the second avoidance of her question and gaped at him. "You have? *Every* one? All of them? For months?"

He looked pained. "Now you think I'm a stalker freak."

"No, no!" She laughed and kissed as high as she could reach, which was somewhere on his sandpapery chin. "I'm amazed. Flattered. Delighted."

More than that. She was going to float up and bounce around the shower walls like a balloon letting out its air. This connection between them went way back. Even the antagonism in their columns had been part of it. She could see that now. Like those great old movies, *His Girl Friday* and *Pillow Talk,* where the hero and heroine fought and bickered to deny their true and growing feelings.

Yet all the while he'd been sneaking out to act on her recommendations. *All* of them.

"You have great taste, Ms. Lowbrow."

She tipped her head coyly. "I like you, don't I?"

"Will I be the subject of your next column?"

"Oh, yes." She paused thoughtfully as she composed the perfect review. "'For those of you hankering after a tasty hunk of beefcake, hanker no more. Proceed to Five Twenty-Three Hilltop Lane in West Chester and feast upon the finest quality male this reporter has ever had. Perfect buns. Plenty of meat. Many condom-ents available. The pleasure will make you want to come again.'"

His laughter rang out in the tiled room, the first time she'd heard him really let loose. The sound made her laugh, too, and feel the world could not become any more perfect than it was just then. It had better stay that way for once.

"I won't even try a response." He let out a last chuckle. "Anything after that would be lame copycatting."

"Thanks." She couldn't seem to smile hard enough.

He opened the shower door and helped her into the warm—even the tile floors felt gently heated—but mysteriously not steamy bathroom. There must be some state-of-the-art dehumidifying gizmo installed. Imagine not having to put up with even the smallest of life's inconveniences. The idea still made her a little queasy.

He dragged his towel over his body, which was so beautiful she felt it impolite not to stare. "So you want to know what my favorite article was of yours?"

"Of course."

"The one about the Lone Star Diner in South Philly."

"You went there?" She couldn't begin to imagine him among the eclectic assortment of South Philadelphians.

"One of the worst entrées of my life." He hung his towel on the rack, took hers from her shoulders and hung that, too.

She arched an eyebrow. "Considering what you have to compare it to, that could still be a compliment for most people."

"Ouch." He handed her a clean T-shirt. "Touché. However, you were absolutely right about the pie."

"Apple?"

"Best I've ever had anywhere."

"Yes!" She grinned and pulled on the shirt, bubbling with excitement. Most of her friends didn't get her deep love—nearly worship—of good food. Even Daphne, who'd grown up in a middle-class Italian family which ate very well, didn't get her obsession. And judging by what Hannah was fed growing up, her parents didn't even inhabit the same dietary planet. "Isn't it incredible? Not too sweet, plenty of apples, minimal goo. They use brown sugar I'm sure."

"Maybe some maple, too."

"That perfect touch of nutmeg with the cinnamon."

"And ginger."

"And the crust…oh my God, it could inspire its own religion."

"The Church of Crust? You were right about all of it. *And…*" he patted his stomach "—about the egg rolls at Ken Han's."

"Yes!" She was practically salivating, not only from hunger but from the thrill of being able to share her passion. "You can taste the individual ingredients in the filling, unlike normal egg rolls."

"Which taste like salty cabbage."

"Exactly."

"You know…" He waggled his eyebrows. "I think I'm getting turned on."

Hannah burst out laughing. "I know! I know. It's crazy."

"Not to mention hungry. Are you? I don't know what time it is, practically evening, I bet."

"I am hungry, believe it or not. Even though all we've done is eat and…that other thing."

"So…what's your point?"

She giggled. "Nothing. Not a thing. Two of my favorite activities."

"Same here. Let's get our traveling circus on the road."

He rewrapped her ankle and helped her on with his sweats, while she was, very uncharacteristically, too full of happiness to speak. Look what they shared. And look how he respected her opinions, even though his true love was food produced on a much different plane.

"I need to take you to some of the places I discovered around the city." He helped her carefully into the wheelchair.

"I'll have to go incognito or lose my reputation." She was glad he couldn't see her face. He'd take her *places*. Places was plural. Which meant he planned for them to go out more than once. Even though he was moving. Or maybe he'd change his mind and stay. Maybe he'd keep the house. Maybe someday they'd have mini-Dereks and mini-Hannahs who could play their hearts out in the rooms upstairs, bring them back to life.

Okay. She was getting ahead of herself again. "I'll dress up. No one will recognize me looking fancy."

"Anyone who saw you in that red dress would. No man could forget a woman like that. Ever."

Hannah laughed so she wouldn't cry at the reverence that showed through his teasing. "Why, thank you, sir."

"You're most welcome." He wheeled her back through the bedroom and toward the elevator. "I didn't advertise who I was at your greasy spoons, either."

"Dark glasses…mustache."

"Trench coat, floodwater pants, sneakers with dark socks."

"Hot, hot, hot."

They did the elevator routine again and arrived back in the kitchen, the scene of the previous night's crime of overeating. Tonight she was in the mood for something simpler. Easier on the stomach and the ethics.

"You know what there is in the cupboard. What sounds good?"

"Well…"

He turned at her less-than-enthusiastic voice. "Something entirely different?"

Hannah decided right then that there was nothing in the world sexier than a man who could read her mind. "I'd like to cook for you, will you let me?"

He looked surprised, then nodded. "You're on. If your ankle can take it."

"It can. And after all—" she smiled sweetly "—I can probably figure out where things are as well as you can."

"Um, yeah. About that…" He rubbed his chin. "I never needed to know my way around a kitchen so I never learned. A terrible flaw."

"Terrible."

"But how about since you're incapacitated, you tell me what you need and I'll find it. Somehow."

"It's a deal. Eggs?"

He found them. And went on to find bread and everything else she called out…eventually. Preparing the meal was the most fun she'd ever had in a kitchen. Sometimes it took them a while to locate something, and drawers and cabinets would be opened and closed all over the room until his shout of triumph would crack them both up. Hannah stood, with his gallant help, to do the cooking, ogling the sleek high-quality pots, and tentative around the flat-topped induction range that heated instantly in contact with the cookware. *The Future Is Now: My Day as Judy Jetson.*

She'd grown up using her mom's temperamental electric range and random-temperature oven to prepare meals when her parents were out or out of it. Amazing what you could do when you mastered an appliance. And when you had no other choice.

The meal was one of her comfort-food favorites, grilled cheese, tomato and ham made with french toast instead of plain bread, honey mustard and a sprinkle of oregano. Add to that a big pot of strong coffee and bananas sliced with a drizzle of cream and a touch of vanilla and cinnamon. Of course, in his kitchen, the bread was artisanal, the cheese was Gruyère rather than Swiss, and the cheddar was encased in black wax and imported from England, not plastic-wrapped in Wisconsin. The tomatoes were fancy vine-ripened ones with actual flavor, and the oregano he disappeared to snip, fresh from the herb garden in the greenhouse. Coffee came, no doubt, blended from beans picked personally for his family. Bananas, thank goodness, were bananas.

But so much for true lowbrow.

She had to admit, however, that the sandwiches were pretty spectacular, the perfect melding of her lowbrow and his highbrow tastes. And judging by the way he inhaled his and made another one on his own, following her instructions, he'd enjoyed them, too. Which satisfied her even more deeply than knowing he'd taken advantage of the recommendations in her column and online. This was something close to her, made with her own hands, part of her past. And he'd not only accepted it, but loved it, too.

Most importantly, as they talked, it turned out they had everything in common except income levels. They liked the same movies—oldies and indie films, occasional action flicks and comedies, but no horror or gore—took the same shots at the same politicians, had read many of the same books and had similar reactions.

Should she perhaps pinch herself? This whole day-night-day had started to feel like a dream. All those years beating herself up for not being cautious enough with men, for trusting too much, for falling too quickly—she'd done all those things here, once again, but what a difference it made when she'd found the right man and they'd dived in together.

"Did you ever have a pet? I bet it got lonely for you in this house." She looked around, frowning. "I know you don't have one now. No pet hairs, no fuzzy mice, no slobbered-on tennis balls."

"That's what the house needs. Fuzzy mice and slobber." He waited for her to stop laughing. "I had a dog as a kid. Toby. Short for Toblerone—like the chocolate. Needless to say, he was a chocolate Lab."

"Of course he was." She grinned. "Is he still around or…no, probably not."

"Long gone. He was a great dog. I have pictures somewhere of the two of us."

"Can I see?" She contained most of her eagerness and still sounded overexcited. She'd bet Derek was positively edible as a child. "I mean when you've finished your coffee."

"Sure. I even know where they are…probably. My dad bought Toby for me, I think mostly to drive my mother crazy."

"How sweet."

"Wasn't it. Toby was great company." He scooped the last of the cream from his bowl and set the spoon down, stared into his coffee, looked up a couple of times as if about to say something, then stood abruptly and took their dishes to the sink.

Hmm. Something about the conversation must be making him uncomfortable. Like… She had no idea. Did he miss his dog that much?

"Your turn." He squirted dish soap into a mixing bowl and ran warm water into it. "Did you have a dog?"

"My parents didn't want the hassle. They could barely feed themselves and me, and could barely get up and out of the house every day. Sometimes they couldn't even do that." She took a sip of coffee to ease the tightness that still cropped up in her throat.

"You had to grow up early."

"I did." She spoke matter-of-factly, as he had. It was incredible to be able to talk to someone who really understood. "As did you."

"I had Rita and Ray."

"And I had Mrs. Babbidge who lived next door. When things got…loud at my house, she'd knock and invite me over for cookies or to watch TV with her. She was like a grandmother."

"I'm glad you had that." He held her eyes, started to speak again, then turned back to the dishes.

Um… So… She finished her coffee and limped over to give him her cup, grabbed a linen dish towel over his objections, and helped dry. What was it he found so hard to say? She was too chicken to ask.

He finished the last dish, rinsed, and handed it to her, dried his hands slowly on a blue-and-white striped towel, then threw it down and cleared his throat, bracing his hands on the counter. "I was thinking…"

"About?" She waited, reminding herself to breathe. If he dumped her, she'd have a mental breakdown. If he said he loved her and had decided not to sell the house, she'd have a mental breakdown, too. Only the good kind.

"Here. So your ankle doesn't get tired." He insisted she sit back on the counter stool, then sat next to her, took her hand and played idly with her fingers. "I was thinking that I'd like to do something for you."

"Okay." That didn't sound like prelude to a dumping, did it? "Does it involve food or sex?"

"You might thing it's better."

"Better than food or sex?" Her heart leapt at a few romantic possibilities, all of which she knew were ridiculous. "I am not sure I'm ready for this."

"How would you like an interview…" He watched her warily. "With Jack Brattle. For real this time."

Hannah's mouth opened, her eyes shot wide, a caricature of the surprise she was feeling genuinely. "Who? Whah? You know him?"

"Yes."

"Oh my gosh." Heat flooded her cheeks. She felt near tears. "I'm…I don't know what to say."

"How about 'sure, that'd be good.'"

"Sure. Yes. Sure. *Thank* you. That would be…way more than good." She took his hand in both of hers and hung on for dear life. This was completely unexpected. Completely…unreal. She wouldn't even have to make up a clever headline because that one would speak for itself: *Interview with Jack Brattle by Hannah O'Reilly.* "What…made you want to do this for me? I mean, before you could have but didn't, and now…"

"It's about trust."

"Trust. Yes. Okay." She took a deep breath, still feeling that this was slightly surreal. "You mean you need to trust I won't tell anyone you know him?"

"And that you'll respect his privacy in what you do write."

"Of course. Of *course.*" At this point she'd only write about his shoelaces if that's what he wanted. Derek knew Jack Brattle! Were they neighbors? Very possible. Or maybe rich people just knew each other. Bumped into each other incessantly at parties in Paris. Maybe their families had done business together, which would mean Derek's family did something related to real estate development. "So…when? I mean where is he? I mean what kind of interview, phone or…"

She hardly dared hope.

"In person. When is good for you?"

"Wow. Wow." She laughed simply because she couldn't keep the emotion back. "Is he in town? Next week? Monday?"

"I'll…check and let you know."

"Wow. *Wow.*" *Stop saying wow, Hannah.* "So…you'll just call him and ask? Just like that?"

He chuckled and touched her cheek with the hand she wasn't squeezing the blood from. "He has a phone just like us mortals."

She loosened her grip. "Okay, yes, I know, sorry. I'm a little…starstruck."

"Hmm." He narrowed his eyes, and she got the impression he meant to tease her, but the look didn't quite come off. "You're going to make me jealous."

"Oh, no. I mean…no way." She shook her head emphatically. "I just want him for his story. You I want for…everything else."

"Make sure it stays that way." His grin seemed halfhearted. His eyes were no longer bright.

She searched his face with concern. Something about this wasn't right. "You're sure this is okay? I mean…you're not going to be calling in some favor you'll need for yourself later?"

"It's fine." He still looked odd. Nervous, but something else, too. He couldn't possibly think she'd fall for Jack Brattle, could he? How many gorgeous rich guys could a woman fit into her life? One was plenty for her. This one, and only this one.

He removed his hand from hers and stood. "I'll go look for those pictures now."

"I'd love to see them." She really didn't like that he was leaving the room so suddenly. "You're sure everything is good?"

"Everything."

"Derek."

He turned back, eyebrows raised questioningly.

"Can I…tell my friend Daphne? She's a reporter and knows about keeping quiet. I'd just love her to know because we're close and…she'd understand what this means to me."

"If you trust her, then it's fine." He walked back toward her, taking his phone out of his sweats. "Because I trust you."

She beamed, sure there were more hearts shooting out the top of her head.

He put the cell on the counter. "Go wild."

"Thank you. So much." She watched him walk out of the kitchen, hoping he'd tell her soon what was bothering him. If something about her interviewing Mr. Brattle would cause him trouble, even she would think twice. But he wouldn't offer if he didn't want her to have the story. Would he?

She dialed Daphne eagerly on the familiar BlackBerry keypad. Luckily her friend picked up immediately.

"Daphne, hi, Happy New Year."

"Hannah? Where are you?" She sounded worried, and her voice was thick, as if she'd come down with a cold. "I've been calling you all day. You didn't answer your phone or your cell."

"I'm not home. I went to check out the Jack Brattle tip."

"Today? In this weather?"

"No, last night."

Her friend gasped. "And you're still not home? What happened?"

"Oh ho *ho* what *didn't* happen." She swirled luxuriously on the stool and nearly whacked her ankle on the kitchen island.

"Hannah." Her friend's exasperation was all too obvious. "Cut the drama. Did you find his house?"

"Yup."

"And? You're not still there, are you?" Another gasp. "Was someone home? Was *he* home?"

Hannah took pity on her poor not-in-love-with-the-perfect-millionaire friend and told her the story. All of it. Well, almost all of it. The roses belonged to her.

"Hannah, Hannah, Hannah." Her friend didn't sound as dreamy and excited as she was supposed to. In fact she sounded exasperated all over again. "You're telling me you're in love *again?*"

"But this time—"

"With a man you met *yesterday* who lied to you and manipulated you into his house and bed?"

"Daphne, it's not like that."

"You didn't meet him yesterday?"

"I did, but—"

"He didn't lie?"

"Well, he…not any more than I did."

"And he didn't manipulate?"

"Look, we've been over this. I mean he and I have. It's water under the bridge—we've gotten past it. I trust him."

"Hannah, honey, this plays like an old tune. You trusted Mr. Can't-Keep-It-Zipped Norberto. Remember what you said? 'I just know this is right, Daphne. This one is going to—'"

"That was different."

"Aw, Hannah. You said that, too." She was trying to keep her tone gentle, but Hannah could hear the frustration.

"I know. I *know*. But this time..." She rolled her eyes. "Forget it. I know you won't believe me. And I guess I don't blame you. But listen, there's more."

Her friend sighed. "I'm not sure I want to hear this."

"Ha ha ha." Daphne must have some serious cranky hangover going at the moment. If anything would get her out of her bad mood, this would. "Get this. He is going to get me an interview with Jack Brattle. For real this time."

"Oh, really." To say her enthusiasm was lacking would be a major understatement.

"I'm serious! This is huge."

"Hang on." She blew her nose, cleared her throat. "Do you have proof he knows Jack Brattle or has access to him?"

"Geez, you believed *Dee-Dee,* why can't you believe him?"

"Well...don't you think it's a little too coincidental? Two offers of Jack Brattle in one day? From your professional nemesis who elaborately planned to humiliate you in print? I'm sorry, but this guy makes me nervous."

"Daphne, listen..."

"Think about it. When was Jack Brattle's last interview with the press?" Her voice rose and started shaking. "Let me think. Last...never. But this guy, who has already lied to you once, is going to produce the man himself on a silver platter and hand him over on bended knee, just because you asked him to?"

"I didn't ask him to. He offered."

"Hannah." She spoke more calmly, trying to be nice to her clearly insane girlfriend. "Jack Brattle has guarded his privacy ferociously for the past decade since his family imploded. How likely is it that this guy has that kind of power?"

"He said it, and I believe him." She put her elbow on the counter, leaned her head in her hand. She did believe him. She did. But it sounded so lame out of context like this. Her temple started pounding.

Daphne sighed again. The sigh of a long-suffering friend. "When is this miracle going to happen?"

"Next week."

"Has Mr. Jack Brattle confirmed this? Within your hearing?"

"It's New Year's Day." She suddenly felt terribly weary, her stomach a bit sick. "Derek can't call him now. Give me a break, Daphne. I know I've screwed up in the past, but you need to trust me this time. You can't keep treating me like I'm some kind of idiot."

A long silence, and a soft hiccup. Was she crying? Hannah's body tensed in alarm.

"Daphne? What's wrong?"

"Paul." A broken sob. "His New Year's Day present was to dump me. After three years."

"*Dump you?* But Daphne…" She struggled for words, found none that fit. "Men don't leave *you*."

"This one did." She barely got the words out.

"But why? I mean what did he say?"

"He was tired of me expecting him to jump. I never thought I was doing that. I mean I…I don't know, I guess I screwed up. He was pretty angry. I just thought after three years… Well, you want to talk about trust? I thought I could trust in what we had."

"Oh my God, I'm so, so sorry." Tears came to Hannah's eyes. She knew what that felt like. No wonder Daphne was so cynical. "Are you home? When the roads are plowed I'll come right away."

"No. I want to be alone." Her voice was so low and miserable Hannah had to turn up her phone's volume. "I'll call you tomorrow. I just need to cry now."

"Daphne, no, don't—"

The line clicked off. Hannah gritted her teeth, feeling her friend's pain. The last thing Daphne needed was to hear Hannah bragging about her new man when Daphne's had just kicked her in the teeth. Hannah needed to call back and apologize.

She started to key in the shortcut for Daphne's number when her phone started vibrating. Good. Daphne, calling back. "Hello?"

"…Who is this?" The voice was female, older, unfamiliar and a bit harsh. Hannah barely stifled a sound of annoyance. She should have checked the number.

"Hannah. Who is this?"

"Where is Jack?"

She rolled her eyes. At least this would be quick. "You have the wrong number."

"No. I don't. Where is he? He hasn't answered all day."

"Uh…sorry, but this isn't his number. Why don't you check—" Hannah froze, realizing her mistake. The phone wasn't hers; it was Derek's. She'd been so upset by Daphne, and his phone was so much like hers, she'd forgotten.

"I'm quite sure it *is* his phone. I'd like to know why *you* answered."

Her stomach grew sicker. Her skin grew clammy. "Did you say…Jack?"

"*Yes.* Where is he? Has something happened? Are you at the house with him?"

Hannah slumped onto the counter, the granite cool under

her hot forehead. The call was for Jack. She didn't need to ask for his last name.

"Answer me." The voice had grown sharper, more suspicious. "Where is Mr. Brattle and what are you doing with his phone?"

10

DEREK STARED MOODILY into his closet. He knew exactly where to find the pictures of Toby. The only things he'd kept from childhood were jumbled in an Adidas shoe box that sat on the far right of the upper shelf, next to his shoe-polishing kit. Inside were the pictures; his lucky pebble, found when he was six and imbued by him with powers for reasons he could no longer remember; his ninth-birthday card from his grandma, which arrived the day after she died; the bouton-niere Amy gave him for the spring dance at Oberlin; the stub from his first paycheck from Brattle, Inc.... Other stuff, too, he couldn't remember the rest.

But he still hadn't taken the box down. Because if he took it down he'd have to go back to the kitchen and face his failure with Hannah. He'd fallen in love for the first time in over ten years, and managed to screw it up in as many ways as he possibly could before twenty-four hours had passed.

Offering her the interview with Jack Brattle was the right thing to do. Failing to mention at the same time, given what she meant to him and what he hoped he was starting to mean to her, that *he* was Jack Brattle was a terrible idea.

How could he explain the pain involved in opening up that part of his life to her, or to anyone outside of the very few who knew of his twinned existence? Since childhood, as a boarding school student and as an employee of Brattle, Inc., he'd been Derek Gibson, for security reasons and to avoid charges of nepotism as he worked his way up.

Now "Derek Gibson" was Mr. Brattle's personal representative, charged by the reclusive hermit himself with the power to run his family's company. A few people knew; there were always risks. But the way his parents had controlled and isolated him in his youth, the way he'd controlled and isolated himself since they died, plus a little luck, meant so far no one had blown his cover. When he'd started to write for *The Herald*, he'd taken still another identity to avoid any connection between his writing and the Brattle company and name.

How could he explain that encountering Hannah's columns and blogs had brought to the surface what must have been a suppressed yearning to connect with someone, with life, with at least a piece of the world as his true self. How could he explain to someone so full of the joy of life that he'd chosen to live so long without it?

And how could he explain how excruciatingly difficult it was, after a lifetime of self-protection, to offer himself up now, even as his certainty had only grown over the last months and finally this last incredible day, that this was what he wanted with her. Even offering the interview while she still thought of him as Derek had been tough. Like a turtle emerging from its shell, he felt he'd be left with no protection. Taking that last step, leaving the shell completely behind by confessing who he was had been too much all at once. Stupidly, he'd panicked.

The public eye had tortured his family, eventually driven his father to emotional ruin and early death, and his mother to suicide. Not hiding anymore, not his past, not his present, not his future…he knew it was what he wanted for his and for Hannah's sake, but he hadn't expected the habit of holding himself close and safe to die so hard.

People would look. People would talk, most people would move on eventually to the next celebrity *du jour*, but many people wouldn't. Until his father's betrayal by a man he'd always considered his best friend, Derek's dad had relished the public role, relished the world's attention. Jack had always hated it. So much so that he'd spent his life denying who he was.

He reached for the shoe box, cradled it in his arms without opening it. The pictures would still be in there. He'd taken them with his own camera, had Rita take the ones of him and Toby together. After they'd been developed, he'd shown them to Rita and Ray and maybe his parents, he couldn't remember. No one else had seen them or moved them, he was sure.

On his way out, he closed the closet door so the light would go out. Step by step he crossed the room. Fear of losing his privacy wasn't the only reason he was anxious. Hannah would have every reason to be furious that he'd held back his identity—again. He'd told the truth when he said he was Jack, told the truth again that he was Derek, and now would tell the truth that he was both. But from her perspective…three lies, not even counting the D. G. Jackson pseudonym. Last time he'd confessed she'd bolted. This time…she couldn't run physically, but she might not be willing to listen to his explanation, to try to understand what his bizarre life had been like.

More than that, while he was indulging in useless pessimism, anyway, Hannah hadn't made it a secret that his fortune bothered her. How would she feel knowing he was not only obscenely wealthy, but part of a notorious family doomed to be in the public eye?

He started heavily down the stairs. Obviously he'd soon find out. His feelings for her had grown to the point where any type of deception had become impossible. And finally, gratefully, he was sick of hiding, sick of lying, sick of being ashamed of who he was. Ready to open himself up to her, he could only hope she wouldn't immediately shut him out.

Hearing a noise at the bottom of the landing, he paused and looked outside. Darkness had come, but the outdoor lights shone through the still air. The snow, slowing for a while, had now stopped completely. The noise grew louder, the hum of an engine. The man Ray had hired to plow the driveway must have started, which meant the roads were passable. Rita and Ray would return to check on the house and on him. There would be nothing keeping Hannah here. After what he'd put her through, and what he was about to put her through, without the storm keeping her prisoner, Derek, Jack, D.G....all of him might not be enough to stay for.

He took a deep breath and moved on to the kitchen. She would have called her friend by now, her friend would be thrilled about the Brattle interview, and her excitement would have buoyed Hannah up even higher. Now he got to burst that bubble hard.

How had he allowed this to happen?

Easy. He didn't know he was going to fall in love with her, and he didn't realize to what extent he was a shutdown prisoner of habit. And something of a coward.

He turned the corner into the kitchen, holding up the box, smiling as naturally as he could. "I found the—"

The smile dropped off his face.

"Hannah." He walked toward her, tossed the box aside on the counter, shocked at the sight of her tearstained face. "What happened, what's the—"

"Don't." She held up her hand and he stopped on the other side of the island, aching to touch her. "Here's your phone back."

He took it, fear keeping him speechless. What had happened? Illness? Accident? Death? Her parents? Her friend?

"You got a call while you were upstairs. I was confused since our phones are so similar and I answered it."

"No problem." His fear started turning sick. "Who was it?"

"A woman. She wanted to know where you were. Apparently it's not like you not to answer calls right away, and with the storm and you having been out last night…"

"Rita." He guessed what was coming, but couldn't process it, as if his brain was protecting him from the bad news for as long as possible.

"She was very worried about you…" She turned her head finally; her eyes were wounded and hostile. "*Jack.*"

He didn't flinch. He deserved this. He was going to get it one way or another, though he desperately wished he'd been able to tell her himself. "Yes. Jack Derek Gibson Brattle. My mother's maiden name was Gibson. My grandmother's maiden name was Jackson, which is why I chose it for the column."

"Ah." Her face crumpled, then hardened. "All in the family. How sweet."

His eyes didn't leave hers. "I was going to tell you. Just now in fact. I went upstairs to get the pictures because I needed to figure out how I—"

"Please. Give me some credit."

He said nothing. He wouldn't have believed himself, either. "Hannah—"

"Remember how you told me no one in your family was normal?"

He put his hands far apart on the counter, leaned forward. "You need to let me—"

"Because I was thinking… You told me about the uncles and aunts—the pervert, the slut and the psycho. Your father was a closeted homosexual with a preference for teenagers, ruined when his best friend outed him, and your mom was clinically depressed and eventually ended her own life."

"Please." He clenched his teeth. Even now it hurt hearing his parents' tragedies discussed as gossip. He knew she was trying to wound him. He hated that she'd succeeded so well. "Don't go there."

"Then *you* came along." She pointed at him, a Salem towns-person accusing a witch. "And you chose 'compulsive liar'? Am I right? Maybe 'drug addict' was too clichéd for a Brattle."

He bowed his head, reminding himself to be patient. Reminding himself what she'd been through in the past twenty-four hours, how often he'd raised her hopes and how often she felt he'd disappointed. "This might be a technicality, but—"

"Just out of curiosity, was *anything* you told me true?"

"Everything was. I told you I was Jack Brattle. I am. I told you I was D. G. Jackson. I'm him, too. I also run the Brattle company and live for the most part as Derek Gibson."

"Oh, right. Of course. Derek Gibson, Jack Brattle's right-hand man. You knew I might piece the whole story together, so you couldn't even tell me that."

"Hannah, it sounds ludicrous, I know, but this is my life and has been for—"

"You know the story of the three blind men who have hold of three different parts of an elephant and each describe a completely different animal? You didn't bother to show me the big picture." Tears started flowing again; she fought them so bravely he wanted to wrap her in his arms and protect her from any pain ever again. Instead he got the box of tissues from beside the sink and placed them within her reach. "But then maybe it's all my fault, like Daphne said, for trusting again."

"She said this was *your* fault?" He made a sound of derision. "Nice friend."

Hannah jerked her head up. "*She's* trying to protect me. Which is much more than you did. I thought you were different. I can't believe I fell for that fairy-tale love-at-first-sight bullshit *again*. Daphne was right. She was right. I need to become a nun."

He was helpless in front of her grief, knowing he caused it, knowing she had every right to be furious. Like a wounded animal lashing out at people trying to help, she was in no position to hear anything he had to say that could make it easier on her. All he could do was weather the storm, wait until she calmed down, and then hope for the chance to explain.

"I called Triple A." She blew her nose, reached for another tissue. "They'll be here as soon as they can."

"No." He drew his hands together on the counter, stood straight. "I need to explain. We need to work this out."

"It's simple. You got what you wanted, I got betrayed and disillusioned."

"I didn't get what I wanted."

"No? What, I didn't give you a blow job?"

"Not fair."

She ducked her head, nodded reluctantly. "No. It wasn't. I'm sorry."

"Look, I know you've been hurt. But this has nothing to do with whatever the other guys' problems were."

"I don't want to hear this."

"You need to. Blocking out trouble, running away from it, isn't the way to—"

"Why not, it's the only thing I haven't tried. And it's what you did."

"So I know what I'm talking about. Shutting people out feels safe, but it isn't really living. The way you put yourself out there again and again, Hannah, with articles, restaurants, your family, your relationships…is how you should live, how everyone should. With enthusiasm and, yeah, a few risks. You inspired me." He studied her face for any sign that she was taking any of his words in. "You brought me back to life."

"Oh, that's ironic. Because now I want to kill you."

He laughed bitterly, he couldn't help it. And his heart rose when he saw she was laughing, too, though through her tears.

"Hannah." He touched her sleeve. "Don't go yet. Let Triple A rescue your car, and I'll drive you home later."

"Why?" She turned to face him, and he hated the dull blank pain in her eyes. "So you can tell me I don't know all the facts? So you can tell me, 'No, it wasn't *like* that. I know how it seems, but if you'd just listen I can *explain…*'"

He gritted his teeth. That was exactly what he'd been going to say.

"I've heard it all before." She wiped her eyes, blew her nose again, calmer now and resigned. He couldn't stand this. "I've been in this situation before. Though you're more creative than most."

"I am not those other men, Hannah."

"No. You're worse."

"I'm not sure I want to know, but how?"

"Because." She ducked her head again, nervously rubbed one thumb over the other. "Because I really, stupidly, thought I was in love with you."

He understood what people said when they claimed to be melting. His heart was a runny mess in his chest. He wanted to touch her, embrace her, carry her back up to his room and make love to her for the rest of their lives. Even in this much pain he was ten times more alive than he'd been for too many years.

I really, stupidly, think I'm in love with you, too, Hannah. He couldn't say it. What had been easy in the greenhouse was impossible now.

"It's a start. Not an end. Just give me time to—"

"No." She carefully got down off the stool and limped toward the door. "I forgave the first deception. I was willing to overlook the fact that you slept with me without telling the truth. But fool me once, shame on you, fool me twice... I can't forgive this time. At least, not this soon. Maybe not ever."

"Hannah..." He felt like a helpless fool. Was this what love was? Would he rather have this pathetic vulnerability and pain than peace and control? If it meant knowing Hannah, then yes. "Don't turn your back on everything that happened between us. Remember the dinner, the dancing, the greenhouse..."

"You can't get me with nice words and flowers now. You can insist you told me the truth all along, but you know what you did." She waved a hand at him, as if he was a bug she wanted out of her face. "I'm not going to argue because I'm terrible at it, and guys always manage to confuse me and make me feel like *I'm* the one who is messed up."

"Oh. So Daphne's a guy?"

He was lucky Hannah only scowled at that comment. But Daphne was not currently on his list of favorite people if she'd made Hannah feel this situation was her fault.

"You didn't deserve what I did. Or didn't do. But I had reasons, and I want you to understand them because of...how I feel about you. And how you feel about me. And because..." His throat cut him off completely. The romantic in him needed more practice with her, especially when she was angry at him. Years and years of practice. Maybe a lifetime. "And because of...what I want us to have...together."

"Us? Which us? Which am I paired with? D. G. Jackson the journalist? Derek Gibson the CEO? Jack Brattle the recluse? Or all three. Is a foursome even legal?" She shook her head in disgust and limped out of the kitchen.

He was after her immediately. "Don't tell me you're going to run outside again."

"I'm going to find my clothes and coat, my shoes and my purse. And wait for the truck. And not talk to you." She stumbled going around the corner and steadied herself against the wall, foot lifted, in obvious pain.

In one more stride he caught up with her, bent, and swept her up. "You can do what you want, you can ignore me, you can detest me, but you can't expect me to let you hurt yourself like this."

"No, of course not. Hurting me is *your* job."

He set his jaw, relieved at least that she wasn't struggling. "Put your arms around my neck. You'll be easier to carry."

For a second he thought she'd refuse and was relieved when she conceded, though she acted as if he were a bag of garbage she was forced to embrace.

Even so, holding her body this close, smelling his shampoo in her hair, made him realize all the more searingly what he had and what he might lose. His gut tightened. This, then, was hell, a new one, very private, designed just for him. Finding the woman of his dreams, finally becoming ready to exit the self-pitying closet of grief and anger to experience life again—or maybe for the first time, given his claustrophobic childhood—and now he was in danger of losing her on the verge of getting it all. Sick, sick irony that the caution he felt had saved and guided his life was currently threatening to ruin it.

"Wait here. I'll get your clothes." He set her down on the dark brown suede armchair in the living room and dragged over the small matching footrest his father had never been without. His chair, his footrest, his scotch and his cigar.

Head down, she mumbled thanks, and he lingered for a quick second, wishing for a miracle to undo the damage.

None came. But one idea did…

He turned and grabbed her shoes from the hallway, went up the stairs, three at a time. In his bedroom he gathered her dress, her underwear and purse, then grabbed a tape recorder off his dresser.

Downstairs he found her coat and laid the clothes in her lap, knelt and put his hands on the armrests on either side of her, boxing her in, wishing he could handcuff her to some piece of furniture until she'd hear him out.

"Hannah."

She hardly looked up. His heart constricted. He couldn't stand her looking so deflated and miserable. But at least she wasn't telling him to go away.

Yet.

Hope rose. He turned on the tape recorder.

"I was born in Philadelphia in 1976, the year of the big bi-centennial celebration. My father had troubled dealings with the mob when he was trying to develop a new casino in Atlantic City in the early eighties, and my parents received kidnapping threats against me and became paranoid. We moved a lot, I had private tutors. Hand-selected friends. When I was fifteen, they sent me to boarding school as Derek Gibson, a name I chose. I was a loner, had a few friends, but no one asked many questions. Same in college at Oberlin.

"I worked with and for my dad also as Derek Gibson, from the time I was old enough to read. He trained me to run the company from the bottom up, told only one or two people I was his son. You know what happened to him. He became greedy, careless, made too many business decisions good for the company and bad for towns and for people.

"In the process, he made enemies, including his best friend, and got caught one too many times with much-younger men. The board got sick of the cover-ups and his friend eventually let him fry. My mother was in bad shape at the time and couldn't handle the scandal or the shame. She killed herself when I was twenty-two.

"I took over Brattle, Inc. with a lot of guidance at the beginning, and vowed to repair the damage, not only to the family name, but to the business. I took the company in a new direction, building affordable housing for lower-income families, investing in already existing properties and renovating them. I put millions into a foundation to award down payments to qualified buyers. In doing so, we stopped making so much money, but we're slowly regaining a decent reputation.

"I'm still downsizing my father's empire. I want to sell this house because I don't like the memories associated with it. For the same reason, I wasn't upset when the good business decision to close our Philadelphia office meant I would be able to sever ties here. I'll miss writing the column as D. G. Jackson, but even we Brattles can't get everything we want all the time.

"I had only one steady girlfriend, in college. Her name was Amy. I never told her I had another life. My father warned me over and over, especially during those horrible weeks of his downfall, before his heart gave out, that I should never trust anyone. Anyone. Even a best friend. Because everyone was capable of betraying me. What he didn't tell me was that by not trusting anyone, I'd be betraying myself—who I was and who I wanted to be.

"But I told you, or was about to before you found out in a case of truly crummy timing on Rita's part. Or maybe the bad timing was mine. I don't claim to have played this all right, or any of it right, but everything I did was because of the incredible, unexpected way you came into my house…and into my heart."

He clicked off the recorder.

"That's it. My story." His voice thickened. "Thank you for letting me tell you."

She stayed silent, staring at her clasped hands, but she was no longer crying.

Hope rose further and stayed, hovering. He wanted to tell her he loved her, beg her to stay, to give him another chance, but the words wouldn't come. He still had too far to go before he could put himself out there the way she could. In any case, she deserved to make the decision on her own, unclouded by pressure from him.

She swallowed, the sound audible in the oppressive silence. And still said nothing. He unclasped her hands and put the recorder in them.

"It wasn't much of an interview, Hannah, but it was with the real Jack Brattle. And now it's yours. That, and whatever you saw and experienced here. If you want any more, let me know."

The noise of an engine, then lights through the front windows, orange flashes sweeping the living-room walls, the furniture and Hannah's stricken face. The plow had come and gone. This was the tow truck.

She nodded almost imperceptibly, then rose, put on her coat and limped toward the front door and toward the truck, her shimmering dress trailing in her hand, sparkling when it caught the light. Derek stood and watched her. His noble speech had been too little, too late. The end of his dream, the beginning of his worst nightmare. Hannah was leaving. The house would feel cavernous when she walked out, devoid of light and joy and life. No way could he lie in that big bed tonight without her. Or shower in the master bathroom, or eat in the kitchen. Might as well sleep on the mat on the floor in his crazy uncle Frank's room. Maybe she'd forgive him and come back someday, maybe sooner, maybe later, maybe never. But he couldn't wait around. His life had been on hold for far too long already.

He'd leave in the morning, sell the house as soon as he possibly could. There was nothing for him here now but painful memories.

11

"MEN SUCK." DAPHNE SHOVED another giant spoonful of rocky road ice cream into her mouth. She lay like an ancient Roman in half recline on her bed, wearing a ratty pink T-shirt that said "I Break for PMS" instead of a toga. Her normally perfect curls stuck out wildly in all directions and her makeup free face sported dark puffy circles under her eyes. She looked exactly the way Hannah felt. "They totally suck."

"You mentioned that." Hannah ate another creamy bite from her own bowl. She'd started their self-pity snackfest virtuously two days earlier with carrot sticks, then slid slowly down the slippery slope with pretzels, low-fat potato chips, full-fat tortilla chips with salsa…then guacamole, then sour cream dip. Finally she gave up all pretense and devolved into a fellow contender for world-record consumption of rocky road.

"They suck."

"I know." Hannah sighed, becoming impatient. A good wallow was vital when things got rough, but Hannah's wallowing abilities had their limit, and that limit was now in sight. She'd gone home from Derek-Jack's house, packed an overnight bag, then Daphne had driven her to rent a car, and Hannah had met her friend at her apartment after a trip to the supermarket for emergency rations. They'd cried together, eaten bad frozen pizza, then had a couple of good slumber party evenings, watching movies, eating chocolate and crying some more. Hannah had slept fitfully on a blow-up mattress on the floor, they'd gotten up around eleven each day and started in again.

By now, sitting here in Daphne's darkened bedroom, Hannah had to admit that, gee, watching the Lifetime channel for the third day straight hadn't made her own pain better, and Daphne's certainly showed no signs of slowing. Not that her friend could get over a three-year relationship in forty-eight hours.

Hannah wasn't sure how long it would take her to get over Derek-Jack. Or if she ever would. No one had ever fit her so well right from the beginning—and face it, a beginning was all they'd had, even if it was an incredibly intense one— shared her tastes, her sense of humor, her view of the world. *And* provided the hottest, sweetest, most passionate sex she'd ever experienced.

Just thinking about it warranted another several spoonfuls of ice cream. From a really big spoon—only because she lacked a trowel.

"They want to live their lives the way they want. We're the ones who are expected to adjust." Daphne sniffed loudly and wiped her eyes. "It makes me sick."

"Yeah." Hannah shifted uncomfortably on the floor-level rocking chair, her body aching to get up and go somewhere, do something. Even exercise. Especially exercise. It was too snowy for a jog, but she could stop by the gym on her way home and work off some of this ice cream. Maybe Daphne would run out of complaints, and she could leave.

"Hey, kids, time for dinner." In the latest weepie on Lifetime, the actress kept up a brave front for her children while crumbling inside from the inattention of her workaholic husband. Once again, he'd missed his daughter's important soccer game.

"Have you ever seen a guy reading a relationship book?" Daphne licked the back of her spoon. "I haven't."

"No. Not me." Hannah's ice cream was starting to taste too sweet.

"Me, neither. It's up to women to figure everything out. And if anything bothers us, if we bring up any issues in the relationship, they act like we're just nagging bitches. Like they're perfect the way they are, and we better shut up and appreciate it."

"Right." Obviously Daphne had never heard herself speaking to Paul as if he were her misbehaving three-year-old.

"It's like they're children, and we have to be their mothers."

"Um, yeah." Could she read minds?

"I mean I want kids someday, but I don't want to have to marry one to get others. I've seen my married friends. The wives do everything, are totally stressed out, and the guys sit there like they're entitled to service their whole lives."

Hannah grimaced. She really wanted to be a good supportive friend, but she couldn't summon the requisite amount of bitterness. "Daphne, I don't think they're *all* that bad."

"Of course *you* don't. If there isn't a bright side, you invent one. Besides, what do you know? You've never had a guy stick around after the initial thrill. Trust me, it's a Jekyll and Hyde experience. Freaks you out the first few times, then you expect it."

"If you say so." Touché…to a point. Hannah's relationships never got the chance to dissolve into boredom. They were always chopped off during the bright hopeful beginning. She'd never seen that as a positive thing. The idea of sitting quietly after work, reading or talking with Der— Ahem. Talking with *someone,* appealed to her tremendously. Imagine a relationship free of uncertainty and fear.

"They want you to be cheerful and supportive *and* sexy all the time. The second you let down your guard or get annoyed, boom, they're done, on to the next one. And chances are their next one is five years younger than you with bigger boobs."

"Yeah." She thought Paul had hung in there for a lot longer than a second, not that he communicated his distaste for Daphne's treatment in a healthier way than scowling and saying, "Go to hell."

"Well, I'm done with them. All of them." Daphne struggled to sitting, frowning thoughtfully. "What are my chances of becoming a lesbian?"

"Good. They're good. About zero."

"Ugh." Daphne fell back on the bed. "That's what I thought."

The actress in the sappy movie fell sobbing into her husband's arms. Miraculously after a near-death experience, he'd realized there was nothing more important to him than family and had arrived home a changed man.

"She's an idiot." Daphne scoffed at the screen. "He'll just screw her over again some other way."

Hannah watched the happy couple, trying not to remember how secure and cherished she'd felt in the arms of Derek…Jack…whatever. "I don't know. I think he really learned something."

"Of course you do, Pollyanna." Daphne heaved herself up and took her bowl to the freezer for a refill. "You think life is a Disney movie, happy ending guaranteed."

Hannah bunched her lips, remembering Derek-Jack's disgust at how Daphne made her feel about herself. About as bad as Norberto and other previous boyfriends had made her feel about herself. While Derek-Jack had made her feel…

She let her spoon thwack back into the bowl of melting ice cream.

Much better than rocky road and Lifetime TV and Daphne.

The movie ended. Daphne's bowl was full again. Another movie came on.

"Men *suck*. The next one I meet, I'm just going to shoot on the first date and save myself and the world a lot of trouble."

"Good plan." Hannah was barely able to sound enthusiastic anymore. Her butt kept falling asleep, her stomach was gurgling unpleasantly from too many empty calories, and her head had started pounding.

An hour earlier she'd had a nearly uncontrollable urge to take her BlackBerry—blessedly unharmed by Matilda's tree trauma—into the other room to check for messages. What if he called? Not that she wanted to hear his voice. Not that she'd weaken and forgive him. At least…not now. *No,* not ever.

This was so confusing. On the one hand, she'd sworn her impulsive behavior had gotten her in trouble for the last time. For the last time she'd fooled herself into thinking she was in love with a man she didn't know at all. So instead of rushing headlong into forgiving him just because she missed him and hated this pain, she was very sensibly and maturely…sitting here. With Daphne. Feeling sick. And bored. And empty of all the good feelings she'd experienced when she was with—

Whatever she was supposed to call him.

"And another thing."

"What?" Hannah was barely listening. She had more interesting things to brood over than Daphne's list of grievances against the male gender. There was the promised interview with Jack Brattle, sitting in the tape recorder in her purse. She still hadn't had the guts to listen to it again, in case his voice propelled her toward more rash stupidity. What would she do about the article? Serve him right if she wrote it. She'd blow his cover wide-open and make a name for herself in the process.

Yeah, that was her all over. Stomping on someone she cared about to climb farther up the career ladder.

"Paul probably thinks he's going to march out there and find someone else. Ha! All he's going to find is how good he had it with me. You watch, he'll come crawling back. And you know what I'll say?"

"No. What." During a commercial break, an attractive woman in a perfect house expressed her joy at being able to clean her floors so easily.

"I'll say, 'You had your chance, Romeo, and you blew it. You don't get a second one with me.'"

Hannah turned in disbelief. "You'd really say that if he realized he'd made a mistake? Don't you think that's kind of harsh?"

"Oh, please." Daphne waved her question away. "Don't you think dumping me instead of trying to work things out was 'kind of harsh'? Whose side are you on?"

"I'm here, aren't I?" And starting to wish she wasn't. "Maybe breaking up was the only way he could get your attention."

"It better not be!" Daphne bounced up to sitting, brandishing her spoon. "Because that trick will backfire right up his ass. I've groveled after that man for three years, I'm not doing it anymore."

"Okay." Hannah pushed the soupy brown lump of ice cream around her bowl. Interesting perspective. Not one Hannah agreed with. But maybe all relationships were complicated like that, a jumble of different people's needs and perceptions.

"And if *I'm* being harsh, what does that make you?"

Hannah shrugged. "Harsh, too."

Too harsh? She didn't know. All she knew was that she'd felt so strong and proud leaving him. Finally she wasn't letting a man walk all over her. Finally she was drawing the line in the sand, saying enough was enough. She'd traveled back home with the tow truck guy in a burst of euphoria. Look what she'd done. Look at her! She'd said, *No, you can't treat me this way,* and for once she'd meant it.

And then…

All the doubts had crept in, like creepy bugs in a horror movie that slip into a house while the owner isn't paying attention, and she doesn't notice until there are so many she can't turn in any direction without stepping on one.

The young mother in the latest movie walked silently into her baby's bedroom, picked up the sleeping infant and cradled him—her?—tenderly. Her husband appeared in the frame, craggy and strong, put his arms around her and joined his wife in gazing at their child. Hannah felt tears rising. Would she ever have that?

"Geez, what kind of idiot does a nursery all in white? Those people are in for some serious cleaning bills."

Hannah sighed, wanting to growl. "Come on, Daphne, it's a movie set. Look how happy they are."

"Sure. He probably just finished banging her best friend."

"Oh, for—" Hannah didn't bother going on. Daphne was clinging to negativity like a shield.

The phone rang. Daphne stiffened hopefully, then caught Hannah's eye and forced herself to look bored and annoyed. "Probably Mom."

She shoved herself out of bed and moved more quickly than she had all day. Her gasp told Hannah the call wasn't from her mother.

"God, Hannah, it's him, what do I do?"

Hannah gave her a withering look. Folded like a house of cards. "How about answer it?"

"But what do I say?"

"You were full of ideas a minute ago."

"Hannah, be serious."

"Okay, okay. You don't have to say anything. But you should really listen and really try to understand."

Something inside her twisted. She hadn't given someone that chance quite recently.

"Right. Good. Okay." Daphne smoothed back her hair, moistened her lips, brushed a chocolate chip off her shirt.

"Uh, Daphne? He can't see you…"

"I know, *I know.* I'm just so nervous. Okay. Here I go." She got a good don't-mess-with-me scowl going, put her hand on her hip for an attitude boost and picked up the phone. "What do *you* want?"

Ah, love. Hannah got up, much to her poor butt's relief, and found the remote to turn down the TV. The young wife was screaming at her shell-shocked husband, who, sad to say, *had* been banging her best friend.

Super.

And yet…by the end of the movie the woman would find someone better for her, who would adore her and love her child as his own, allow her to be herself in a way her husband never had. She'd be happier than she'd ever thought possible and would graciously forgive her ex. Of course Cheater Boy and the best friend would be miserable.

Hannah grabbed her purse. Wouldn't it be nice to know that when bad things happened you had a guaranteed happy ending lurking around the corner?

"Oh, Paul." Daphne was crying, but not miserably. "I miss you, too, sweetie."

Hannah snorted, she couldn't help it, and went into the only other room in the apartment. She was glad Daphne and Paul were working things out, but she did not want to hear the rest of Daphne's happy ending.

In the kitchen area's tiny sink, she rinsed out her ice cream, not caring about the waste, and stuck the bowl in the dishwasher. Where was Hannah's happy ending? Where was the wonderful man who would come to her now that she'd learned her lesson about rushing in where intelligent women feared to tread, and gained the strength to insist on being treated with respect?

Sick dread invaded her mood, along with a picture of a certain handsome billionaire tenderly bringing her tea, gently wrapping her ankle, sensually feeding her raspberries...

What if she'd already found him?

Argh! Uncertainty and confusion were the pits. She opened her phone, sparking adrenaline even as she told herself he wouldn't have called, if for no other reason than he didn't have her number.

One missed call...from her parents, who wanted her to come over some afternoon. Hannah's heart sank. Foolish, foolish heart. Would it ever catch up to her brain?

Daphne's giggle sounded from her bedroom. Hannah didn't smirk this time. She had no reason to when she'd been praying for the same call for herself. But it was time to go. Daphne would want to be alone to prepare for all-night nookie.

Just the thought made Hannah want to smack a pillow over her mouth and let loose with a primal scream. Daphne would get fabulous, passionate makeup sex from the guy she loved...and Hannah got to visit her parents.

She called to let them know she'd see them the next day, and stopped in the doorway of Daphne's bedroom to say goodbye to her now-glowing friend, who'd immediately started stressing over what she'd wear after she ran to take a shower, shaved her legs, plucked her eyebrows, put on gallons of damage-control makeup...

"Have fun."

"I will. I always have fun with— Damn, what goes with these pants? I thought that red sweater was clean, crap!"

"So, uh, men don't suck now?"

"No, they most definitely do. But this one loves me, and I'd be an idiot to let him go." She tossed another sweater on the growing reject pile on her unmade bed. "And, well,

Maybe, okay, maybe, he had just the tiniest, teensiest, little point."

"Which was?"

"Maybe I…" She took a deep breath, as if she really wasn't looking forward to the rest of the sentence and just wanted it over with. "…focus too much on what I need and expect him to produce it. It's just that…he used to. And then he stopped. I don't know. Maybe I…"

"At least you'll get to talk it out now."

"Yes." She grabbed a pink top with a nod of approval, trying to hide her happiness. "Where is my black bra? Crap!"

Hannah finally found it in a corner of Daphne's crammed lingerie drawer, after they'd pawed through enough lace, rayon and marabou to outfit an entire catalog.

"So…you'll take him back?"

"Of course I will." Daphne made a sound of exasperation, but nudged Hannah affectionately with her shoulder. "I love him."

"And that's enough?"

"For me, yeah. It is. I know I get, um, a little enthusiastic about what I want to do and what I'd like him to do. He drives me crazy the way he's so different from me. But we're good for each other. I goose him up, he holds me back when I'm going to shoot off somewhere. Almost losing him…" She shook her head and sank on the bed as if her legs could no longer carry her even at the thought. "I guess the cliché is true, that you don't know what you've got until it's gone."

Hannah checked in with her heart, which still felt as if it were roasting over live coals. "Yeah."

"So what about you? What about Jack?"

"I still don't—"

The phone rang. Daphne's face lit and she lunged for it. "Hi, sweetie. No, not ready yet, but I'm hurrying…"

Hannah let herself out, more confused than ever, which she

wouldn't have thought possible. Back home, she ate better, but that was about all that improved. The frustration and indecisiveness continued. By now she was an expert. *Woman Goes for Gold Medal in Brooding.* No luck working on her next Lowbrow column, either. Slept badly, even in her own bed. By afternoon she was dying to get out of the house and practically ran to her car.

Forty-five minutes later, nervous on the still-wintry roads in her rented car, she arrived in Brookhaven and pulled up to her parents' neat suburban ranch, which they'd bought five years earlier with money inherited from Hannah's grandparents. She let herself in with the key they insisted she keep, and found her mother alone in the small living room, sitting with a simple child's puzzle in front of her on a small wooden table.

"Hey, Mom." She bent to kiss her mother. "You look great."

She meant it. Her mother was dressed in black pants and a pink sweater, her graying hair newly colored auburn and recently cut in a flattering chin-length bob. She looked stronger and less pale, much more her old self. Considering she'd barely been able to move after the stroke, it was nothing short of a miracle.

Hannah and her parents had invested a ton of energy and patience getting to know each other again after Mom and Dad quit drinking, and a whole new relationship had blossomed. She could now happily and honestly say she loved and respected them both unconditionally, not just because they were her parents and she had to. Fate had been nasty and unfair threatening her mother. Hannah wanted years and years more to enjoy her new sense of family.

"Thank you, sweetheart." Her mom smiled, eyes twinkling. "You look horrible."

"Yeah, um, thanks." She pushed her unstyled hair self-consciously behind her ears, wishing in a sudden painful burst that Derek-Jack could experience similar family support.

"So…" Her mom shook her head, lips pressed disapprovingly, eyes still smiling. "When did you last look in a mirror?"

"I was at Daphne's for a sleepover. Or two."

"It shows." She smiled at her plump, pretty, brunette nurse, who came in with a tray of tea and cookies. "Thank you, Susie. Now that Hannah is here, why don't you go relax?"

"I'm not paid to relax, Mrs. O'Reilly." She cleared the half-finished puzzle and set a cup of tea and a small plate of cookies on the table.

"With the peanuts we pay you, you'd be crazy not to when you get the chance."

"It's not a problem." Susie turned the cup handle toward Hannah's mother who had been groping at it in some confusion. "The experience is invaluable, and you know the foundation supplements my income."

"What foundation?" Hannah took a bite of the cookie and had to put it down before she burst into tears. Shortbread. 'Nuff said.

"Brattle, Inc."

Hannah nearly choked on her tea. *Brattle, Inc.?* Was the man going to haunt her everywhere she went?

Her mother sent Hannah an alarmed look, then calmed when she saw her daughter wasn't near death from cookie. "Isn't that the foundation that saved your father's orchestra?"

"Yes, it is," Susie said patiently. "We made that connection, remember?"

"Did we?" Her mother frowned. "I don't remember. I don't remember anything."

"That will change."

Hannah couldn't stop staring, first at her mother, then at Susie, while her brain supplied a picture of Jack in the library section of his third floor after he admitted he'd read about her parents in her blog, uncharacteristically awkward and self-conscious. *I'm...glad things are better for your mom and dad.*

No, she was crazy. It was a coincidence, nothing more. "Does...the foundation sponsor a lot of nurses for home care?"

"Not as far as I know." Susie helped Hannah's mother land her cup back in the saucer. "This was a special grant."

"Ah." Hannah needed help putting her cup down, too. She needed help breathing at the moment. "And...did Dad's symphony apply for a grant from the Brattle foundation?"

"Oh, no." Her mother pounced triumphantly. "I remember that. It was remarkable. A check just showed up one day, after the symphony's troubles had been public for years. The management hadn't approached Brattle because the foundation had no history of funding the arts."

Holy Cheez-Its. Hannah didn't know what to say. She was so close to crying she could only sit there and keep her eyes as wide-open as possible, hoping the teardrops would drain before spilling over onto her cheeks, making her look a tad too invested in symphonic welfare. Jack Brattle had read about her parents in her blog and stepped in to save them? Before he'd even met her? It made no sense. He couldn't have done it for her sake all those months ago. And yet...why else would he?

"Susie, I'd like to talk to my daughter for a few minutes, please. She can help me with the cup."

"Of course." Susie glanced curiously at Hannah, who probably looked like a recently dug-up zombie, and left the room.

Hannah took a seat next to her mother on the blue-and-white striped couch her parents had bought the year before, gradually replacing the older worn and grubby furniture she'd grown up with.

"Hannah, I might not be quite back to myself yet, but I still know when you're upset." She held out her hand. "So…? I'm ready to listen."

Hannah took her mother's hand, blissed out by this new relationship between them, and told her the whole crazed up-and-down tale, managing to keep back the pity-me sobs…for the most part.

When she finished, her mom was quiet for so long Hannah was afraid she hadn't been able to take it all in.

"Mom?"

"Yes, dear." She sat peacefully staring at the print of a Hudson River landscape on the opposite wall, as if no one had been talking at all.

Hannah couldn't help mild panic. "Are you okay?"

"Of course." She squeezed Hannah's hand. "I was just thinking."

"About what?"

"That you're a fool."

Hannah's eyebrows shot up. "Well, thank you."

"You are." Her mother managed a sip of tea. Hannah guided the cup back down and handed her a napkin to wipe a drop from her lips. "If you find a man who loves you that much you should hold tight with both hands and never let go."

Oh. The second time in one day. How often did Daphne and Mom dish the same advice? They couldn't be less alike. Maybe Hannah needed to pay attention.

"I have a man who loves me that much, though he didn't know it for too many years, and therefore, neither did I." She frowned, and then turned her once-again lively eyes on her daughter. "Seriously, what is wrong with you?"

"I…" This wasn't exactly the question Hannah was expecting. "I didn't know about the money he gave you."

"It has nothing to do with money. Look what he offered you."

"The interview?"

"Interview." She spat the word out, as if it were a terrible insult. "He offered you his soul, Hannah. Along with his heart."

For a second Hannah wasn't sure her mother was all there. "He…lied to me."

"What would you have done in his shoes?"

"I wouldn't have lied."

"I don't think you can be so sure." She turned toward the painting again, gazing with faraway eyes. "Since you were a girl, your life's been so full of coping with your own whirlwind of feelings and wants that you haven't had enough practice absorbing other people's. I take blame. Your father and I forced you to be selfish because of how selfish we were."

Hannah felt tears threatening again and fought not to withdraw her hand from her mother's warm grasp. "So now I'm selfish as well as naive."

"Naive? Who said that?"

"Daphne. I trust too much and forgive too quickly."

Her mother dismissed Daphne with a rude noise. "Neither trust nor forgiveness are faults if the recipient deserves them."

"But how do you know when—"

"Tell the story again from his point of view, Hannah. Not to me, but to yourself." She squeezed Hannah's fingers again and let go. "You're the one who needs to hear it."

She heard it. An hour later she was speeding toward Jack's house, having listened to his tape on the way home from her mother's, once, twice, three times. Each time she'd tried hard to put aside her hurt, her feeling of betrayal, and to apply what she knew about the man, and what she could guess about his past, to the words she was hearing.

Yippee. Her mother was right. Break out the bubbly, Hannah was a certified fool. Always had been. Her problem wasn't necessarily impetuousness, though that didn't help.

Her problem was the same one she'd accused Daphne of so many times. She was only thinking of herself. With other men it had been all about her fantasy, her ideas of what love should be and how it should carry them both away. With Jack, it was all about her pain, her anger.

Halfway home she'd turned to the northwest toward West Chester. No, she didn't love the way Jack—his name was Jack!—had worked every minute of their time together. But there was no doubt that he had his reasons, good ones from his perspective, even if some of them were still incomprehensible.

He hadn't acted out of disregard for her. He'd acted as she had, to protect himself from the big bad heartbreak wolf—until the end when he'd offered her the interview and therefore even his protection. And in reaction to this so-amazing gesture, she'd taken a giant step backward and fled for safety. What she'd called caution, strength, sanity… Nope. Simply impulsive fear.

Hadn't he admitted she was the only woman he'd ever told about his double life? Hadn't he as good as admitted he loved her? Hadn't his actions backed that up, with his astonishing rescue of her parents and his admittedly odd method of coercing her to his house, then his tender and loving and ver-r-ry sexy treatment of her?

Yes, Mom, she was a fool. But she wouldn't be one any longer. This trip back to his house was completely impulsive, totally spontaneous, and exactly what she should be doing.

She arrived at his driveway as twilight fell, heart pounding, and emerged, shaky-legged, into the icy air, to examine the big iron gate. Locked. Without the storm, however, she noticed something she hadn't seen three—could it really only be three?—days earlier: an intercom at the right edge of the drive, set into the gate.

Anxiously, she pressed the buzzer. And waited. Pressed it

again. Waited some more. Her anticipation started dulling. Excuse me, how dare no one be home and ruin her perfect dramatic moment? She had to—

The machine crackled. "Yes?"

Ha! She wanted to shout her relief. A woman's voice. The same one she'd heard on the phone. Rita. "Hi. I'm Hannah. O'Reilly. I was wondering if Jack was home."

"Oh." She sounded surprised and, unless Hannah was nuts, disappointed. "No, he's gone, dear."

"Gone." Hannah drooped. The first time she was sure spontaneity was the right thing to do, the gesture had been wasted. "When do you expect him back?"

A long pause, during which Hannah could swear she heard the woman sigh. "I'm sorry, dear. I don't."

The words didn't register. "You don't…what?"

"I don't expect him." This time Hannah heard the sigh unmistakably. "He isn't coming back."

12

DEREK STARED AT THE SCREEN on his monitor. He'd pulled up a blank document for his final Highbrow column an hour ago and the page was still virgin-white; his deadline arrived in two hours. Thoughts of the column he'd been originally planning to write about Hannah wouldn't leave him alone. Worse, they kept morphing into thoughts of Hannah that had nothing to do with it. *And round and round we go.*

He got up and went over to his office's huge corner window, stared out at the view of Lake Michigan feeling like a guppy in a fish tank. He wasn't used to being unproductive. Didn't like it at all. But then a lot had changed since that night with Hannah less than a week ago.

A week. Geez. He felt as if he'd been with her for years and without her for a lifetime.

A knock sounded behind him. His new secretary, Amanda, hovered at his open door, carrying a load of files and papers. "Mr. Gibson?"

"Come in." He strode back to his chair, wondering how soon he could book a ski vacation and wondering further how much shock he'd cause if people heard he was actually taking time off.

"I have the Parker letter for signature and the report on the Bixby project."

Derek scanned both while she waited patiently. Amanda was a vast improvement over Mrs. Shelby who had been a lovely woman, but flustered easily and let too many typos through, therefore hadn't lasted long. Amanda was also her physical opposite, tall and thin and young, where Mrs. Shelby had been short and plump and of a certain age.

"This looks fine." Derek sat and selected his favorite pen, from a Cross set his father had given him for graduation from Exeter, signed the letter and handed it and the report back to Amanda. "Enclose two copies of the contract, and let me know when they're returned. The report goes to the board."

"Got it."

"My three o'clock conference call…?"

"Set up, all parties expect to be there. And your reservations for China have been confirmed. First class, aisle seat. Also, Jim Schultz can't make your meeting Tuesday, so I cancelled your trip to Dallas."

"Thank you." He made the note on his computer calendar program, then smiled at her, wondering when smiling would come naturally again. "That it?"

"Oh, Rita called."

"Again?" He'd been tied up in meetings all morning.

"She wouldn't leave a message, just asked you to call when you could."

He nodded, relieved. If there was an emergency she would have asked him to call back immediately. "I will, thanks."

"And these are the documents for the Darrin development which Mr. Brattle has to sign."

"Excellent. I'll see him tomorrow."

"Really?" Her curiosity bordered on unprofessional. "Is he…coming here? To Chicago?"

"No." He sighed. The duplicity he'd lived with his whole life was becoming more and more tedious. He wished Hannah would write up the interview and to hell with the consequences. He'd scanned *The Philadelphia Sentinel* daily since

New Year's, but nothing had appeared. Maybe he had an overinflated sense of his own importance, but it seemed to him if the paper had the article, they'd print it in a big hurry. Which meant Hannah hadn't written it. Why not?

"I'm curious." Amanda coyly started playing with a pencil on his desk. "What does he look like?"

Derek blinked. "Who?"

"Mr. Brattle."

"Oh." He shrugged, annoyed. "About my height. About my coloring and build. Yellow teeth, bad skin, two heads…"

She giggled. "Think I'm his type?"

He would have laughed, but her question didn't seem to be part of the joke, which annoyed him more. "He likes petite blondes with lowbrow taste, no sense of caution and little inhibition."

Her nose wrinkled; she threaded pink-tipped nails through her brown bob. "The hair I could dye, but I don't think I can lose height."

"Not worth it."

"From what I hear he's worth a lot."

Derek wearily repressed a childish impulse to say, Oh, shut up. "He's…involved with someone."

"Lucky girl."

"Why do you say that?" He could barely hide his irritation. This was exactly the type of idiocy he'd avoided successfully for so long. And exactly what he'd be inviting back into his life if he fused Derek and Jack into one person. For one intense moment he hoped Hannah wouldn't write the article. "You don't know him. He could be a complete jerk."

"All that money." She sighed wistfully, flicked the pencil so it rolled across the desk and stopped at his elbow. "Who'd care?"

"Right." He picked up the phone, intending to send the

message that the conversation was over. Luckily she got it, gathered up her papers, and left.

Yeah, all that money. Bought you happiness by the truck-load, didn't it. Hannah's distaste for his wealth was ten times more attractive than the standard worship of it.

He replaced the receiver, shoved back his chair, and clasped his hands behind his head. What was she doing right now? Writing the article? Not writing it? Missing him? Changing her mind about giving him a second—no, third chance?

Nice thought. More likely she was making a Jack Brattle voodoo doll to roast in her oven. He'd wanted to call her only about a thousand times since New Year's Day. But what was the point? If Hannah had changed her mind, if she'd really understood what he was saying on the tape, what he'd said to her in person, she, of all people, was fully capable of coming after him herself. Jack Brattle might be next to impossible to find, but Derek Gibson was in full public view. Her silence meant only one thing: *I don't want you.*

Another glance at the blank Highbrow column—what the hell was he going to write about? Maybe short and sweet was best. "It's been fun, see ya later." Think that would fill enough space?

Nah, he didn't, either. All week he'd been unable to escape into work, exactly like this. From an early age, he'd trained himself to close off everything but the essentials of what he needed to accomplish at any given moment. But even his disciplined mind couldn't combat the power that was Hannah. She'd derailed his whole existence.

He'd trade in all his money for a time machine so he could go back and do everything differently. Lure Hannah into his house, tell her right away he was Jack Brattle, that he knew who she was because—surprise!—he was also

D. G. Jackson, but that he wanted to give her the interview because he knew she'd do a warm, human, intelligent and tasteful job presenting his truth to the world. Then he'd feed her. Take her to bed, then into the greenhouse and tell her he loved her. Kneel at her feet and offer her the rest of his life. The end.

Right. He rolled his chair back up to the desk, a massive, imposing cherry piece of his father's, which right now he'd like to trade for a golf cart or a safari vehicle. What was the point of wishing for things he couldn't have? He'd done that his whole life and should know better. The only relevant point was that he'd made a mess, had been unable to clean it up, and now faced the rest of his life without Hannah. The only question remaining, did he face it as Derek? Or as Jack? The choice had seemed so clear when he was with her.

He picked up the phone again and dialed Rita. Maybe she had news about selling the house. He wanted the entire transaction over with as soon as possible. With the Brattle mansion off his back, he could tackle how best to move forward.

Damn it. Moving forward was supposed to include Hannah. Without her he risked trading the prison of anonymity for the prison of missing her, and with his offer of the interview, the prison of being Jack Brattle, caged in the public eye, with no one around he could trust the way he trusted her.

Staying Derek was looking better all the time.

"Rita, hi."

"Jack, we have a buyer."

"Already?" A jolt of mild panic surprised him.

"She's very excited." Rita's heartiness sounded forced. "Wants to close as soon as possible."

"Really."

"Her house is already sold. She said she fell in love with

yours the second she walked in the door. Big money, moving down to Philly to be closer to her family. I think the husband is one of those early retirement Wall Street geniuses, and they need a way to spend lots of his money."

Derek's brain tried to celebrate without much luck. "I had no idea we'd find a buyer this soon. I'm…stunned."

"Aha!"

Derek narrowed his eyes. "Aha?"

"You don't really want to sell, do you."

He heard himself laughing strangely. "Come on. I've been plotting to get rid of that albatross for years."

"Uh-huh."

His temper rose. "I know what I'm doing."

"And I've known you since you were a boy, so I can tell when you're lying. Don't forget that."

"Yes, ma'am." His sarcasm was harsh, as was the pain in his chest. "I'll keep that in mind."

"Jack." Her voice gentled. "I'm just saying you don't have to do this. It's okay to change—"

"Thanks for the advice."

She sighed and despite his anger, he felt guilty for snapping at her.

"How soon can you come down for the closing?"

"Earliest would be…" He went back to his desk, brought up his calendar on the screen in place of the not-written Highbrow column. "I had a meeting in Dallas cancelled for Tuesday."

"Tuesday. I'll let her know. You'll make the flight reservations or should I?"

"Amanda will make them." He answered automatically while his brain whirled. Selling the house. Launching himself into a new life, one he wanted, one he was inviting, but…unpredictable. He hated not being in control.

Except the night he spent with Hannah.

Come on, Derek. He yanked himself back from useless mooning. Jitters were normal after so long hiding. He'd push through them, give Hannah another week to write up the interview. If it didn't appear he'd decide once and for all either to come out as Jack Brattle by himself or put the matter to rest and commit to being Derek for the rest of his time on earth. The sale of the house was a good thing. The remainder of his plan and his life would soon fall into place.

"One more thing." Rita paused long enough for Derek to get nervous. "A woman named Hannah came to see you."

Adrenaline burned through his system. "When?"

"Last night. I tried to call while she was here, but you didn't answer your cell."

He bit off a curse. If only he'd known… "I was tired, figured you just had a question about the house. What did she want?"

"She seemed very disappointed you weren't here. She asked how to get in touch with you. I nearly gave her the number, but I know how protective you are."

"Right." He wanted to laugh, but it wasn't funny. She couldn't even give his number to the woman he loved. What kind of half life had he lived? "Did she leave her number?"

"No. But she seemed to want to see you awfully badly."

His heart leapt. But then why hadn't she left a number? "Did she mention an interview?"

Silence, not entirely unexpected. "You mean for the job at the foundation?"

"No. Her interview of me."

More silence. Definitely expected. "She's from the *media?*"

"*Philadelphia Sentinel.*"

"But she asked for Jack."

"Yes." He really didn't want to go into this. He just wanted to know if Hannah wanted *him,* or only more details for her rise to fame.

"Okay, Jack. You better tell me everything."

"Did she say what she wanted?"

Rita made a sound of exasperation. "She said she had a few more questions."

His heart sank. Low. Then lower. More questions. For the interview. "I promised her I'd be available. So she didn't leave any way for me to get in touch?"

"You gave her an interview as Jack Brattle?"

"You said she asked how to reach me?"

"What on earth prompted you to—"

"What did you tell her?"

She growled in frustration. "Fine. I won't ask. I told her you'd moved away and weren't coming back."

"Okay." His voice came out sounding half-strangled.

"Is that a problem?"

"No, not a problem."

"This isn't just about an interview, is it?"

"Rita, I really don't want to—"

"You're involved with her. Personally."

"Not your business."

"And you gave her an interview as *Jack Brattle*. Seems pretty obvious there is a problem."

"No. There's no—"

"I bet I know the solution."

"*Rita.*" He put his elbows on his desk, gripping a fistful of hair with his free hand. "I offered her everything. If it was enough she would have stayed."

"Oh, right. The Brattle way. Your conditions, your rules, and if people don't immediately play by them, you cut them off at the knees."

His body turned to stone in his chair. His father's chair. His father's desk. "Excuse me?"

"Just how your dad operated." Typically, she ignored his

warning tone, which usually sent his employees ducking for cover. "Well, let me tell you something about women."

He heard Ray's level voice in the background, Rita shooting something back at him. Derek pictured the two of them: Rita, short, plump and feisty; Ray, tall, quiet and thin. When Derek was a kid, he used to think of them every time he read the poem about Jack Sprat and his wife. "I really don't need to hear this."

"Women can't make snap decisions the same way men can because they think with their heads and feel with their hearts at the same time. They can see both sides of an equation, can absorb larger and more far-reaching implications, while men are good at zipping to the core of a problem and coming to a quick conclusion. I don't judge either way. Both are important.

"But in this case it means you can't take Hannah's initial reaction as her final answer. If asking interview questions was all she wanted, she would have called your office. She didn't. She drove all the way out here and was devastated when she found out you were gone. I could hear it in her voice."

He hated this. The hope Rita was raising and with it the renewed vulnerability and fear. He wanted things calm, ordered, under his control. "Thanks. I'll take that under advice—"

"I'm not finished. You have spent your whole life shutting people out. To the point where people aren't even able to *ask* to come in. This woman wants in, Jack. And you'd be an idiot not to let her. This house is your home. Come make it a home. Take a risk, and let this woman in."

Derek slammed his fist on his desk. For God's sake. He was not a little boy who'd drawn on the walls with crayons. "*Now* are you finished?"

"Yes," she said cheerfully. "So salvage your pride by

hanging up now and telling yourself, 'I'm an idiot.' In the middle of the night when you can't sleep, you can admit I was right, take the house off the market, and call this Hannah person. Even better, transfer me now to your secretary, and I'll have her do it."

He gritted his teeth. If she thought her half-baked psychology would make him toss himself in front of another oncoming Hannah train, she was completely nuts. "I'll do it my way. My risk. The house stays on the market. I'll be there for the closing Tuesday."

She sighed in exasperation. "Okay, Mr. Brattle. See you Tuesday. The buyer sounds like a piece of work. Should be fun."

Right. Fun like a final exam in physics you didn't study for. He stared at the still-blank screen, then at the clock ticking toward his deadline, thinking about his Highbrow column, about Hannah, about leaving Philadelphia, about Hannah, about food and the house, about Hannah, about Hannah…

And he suddenly knew exactly how the article should go.

Highbrow, *The Philadelphia Herald*
Dear readers: Today we bring you D. G. Jackson's final Highbrow column. We at The Herald *wish Mr. Jackson all the best and will miss his humor, insight and talent. Next week we'll start a series on American wines outside of California.*

I've enjoyed writing this column very much over the last three years. Any excuse to explore eating well is worth grabbing. I started with the idea that I could share my passion for good food, maybe inspire a few of you to try some new places, new flavors, new levels of service. Going to the same fast-food or neighborhood restaurant can become a habit. I wanted to challenge people to look beyond the obvious and risk something new. I didn't want this to be preaching to the converted. I hoped to reach people for whom a meal was merely a way to fill the stomach on the way to a movie, and show them that good food is something to be savored, an evening's entertainment all on its own—at its best, an art form.

Given the mail I received from readers, I succeeded with some of you, not others. To be expected.

What I didn't expect was how much I would learn during this process. I learned that aspiring to good food doesn't always mean looking higher, spending more. I learned that focusing on highbrow aspects can be limiting, like wearing blinders. I learned that I was stuck in the same prison and safety of habit as those people who don't venture beyond chain restaurants advertised on TV. The same kind of paralysis can set in at any level.

Judging by my mail, many of you enjoyed the friendly rivalry set up by *The Philadelphia Sentinel* instigation of the Lowbrow column, written by Hannah O'Reilly. I learned from her. I learned to value the perfect grilled cheese sandwich, fresh homemade pie from an all-night diner, perfect pickles from a corner deli. Like the Charlie the Tuna commercials in the seventies, it's not about good taste, but about tasting good.

My hat is off to my formidable opponent. My hope as I wind down this column is that she opens hers, that she joins me in admitting the best of highbrow and lowbrow is when they come together. That true magic happens when grilled cheese is made with Vermont cheddar on *ciabatta* or focaccia. When the apple pie can be a buttery tarte tatin, and the pickles not just cucumbers but mixed vegetables flavored with a variety of herbs. That out-of-season raspberries and pure-butter shortbread cookies can become the love of your life as easily as bananas and Oreos.

That sharing the pleasure with those you love is the real joy and passion of eating and of life.

Lowbrow, *The Philadelphia Sentinel*

Hello, gang, and Happy New Year to all Lowbrow readers. Today's column will be slightly different. I have a new place to review, a place none of you will get to go. It's quite a story and a revelation.

First of all, right up front, let me tell you. I won a few battles, but I ultimately lost the war with the High Priest of Highbrow, D. G. Jackson. He got me so thoroughly that I have to call the contest over and cower in humiliating defeat. Listen and learn.

The setting is New Year's Eve. The bait for poor unsuspecting journalist, Hannah O'Reilly, is the offer of an interview so incredible it would make finding proof of Bigfoot's existence ho-hum, yesterday's news. Off she goes on a stormy night to the assigned place, and what does she find? A near-deserted mansion. A handsome stranger who offers her the meal of a lifetime. Caviar. Foie gras. Prosciutto with fresh figs. A bottle of champagne that would buy her groceries for weeks. What kind of lowbrow could enjoy a meal like this?

Our intrepid reporter betrayed you all. She cheated on you with foodie passion and joy so great that even now she cannot summon the requisite shame. Alas!

But wait, there is hope. Don't hang up your juicy meatball subs and crisp salty hash browns, ladies and gentlemen. Because over the course of the evening, D. G. Jackson confessed—confessed!—to me that he had been a Lowbrow devotee for some time. Imagine!

It's time to rip down borders, dissolve the enmity. Accept the fact that a true foodie is just that. Someone for whom good food is good food, no matter the price, no matter the status. This column will go forward under that umbrella. I'm thinking of calling it Nobrow. Whadya think?

Ending today on a personal note, I thank my colleague

D. G. Jackson for his talent and expertise in his excellent column. I even forgive him for the prank he pulled. Me, the great crusader for lowbrow justice! What he offered to me was far more valuable than the price I had to pay. Over that meal I discovered many new loves that will last me a lifetime. Philadelphia will miss him. So will I. Until next week, readers, whether you go low or go high, make sure you go out and eat!

Live large, live long, live lowbrow. Until next week…

13

DEREK PRESSED HIS REMOTE and the iron gates to the Brattle estate—soon to be the Jansen estate—swung open. He had imagined several times how it would feel to approach his ancestral home—using the term with a certain mixture of irony and bitterness—knowing it would be the last time. He realized that a small amount of grief was normal under the circumstances. Whether or not he'd ever had affection for the house, it did symbolize, along with Rita and Ray, one rare constant in his life, one place where he could be Jack Brattle without fear of discovery. Losing that would understandably involve some pain, pain he would soon overcome when the deed was done, the new owners moved in, and he could look forward to starting over.

No matter what happened after Hannah's article came out—or didn't—he wouldn't be the same man. He'd take more time for himself, spend more time on trips that had nothing to do with business. Choose one place—his condo in Chicago, his house in Dallas or San Francisco—and settle permanently. Try to cultivate a social life. In short, be normal for a change.

He'd found Hannah's home number and called her the day before, left a message on her machine saying he'd be back in town briefly, thanking her for the tribute in her Lowbrow column, saying he was happy to help her out further with the Brattle article. She hadn't responded. Obviously she had worked out whatever questions she'd had and no longer needed any contact with him.

That rejection extinguishing his last foolish hope buoyed by her column was even more crushing since he'd told himself over and over not to try to connect one more time, but hadn't been able to resist.

All the better that he'd be selling the place. If she wanted nothing to do with him, he didn't need the reminders the house evoked of their time together.

The gate closed behind him with a tap on the remote control he'd have to remember to leave here. He'd wanted to hold the closing in his lawyer's office, but the buyer had insisted on having it right here at the house. Apparently she couldn't wait to get her hooks in it.

Fine by him. He pulled up to the front door, sat for a moment, looking out over the still-wintry grounds, the bare trees thickly lined with snow that had fallen the night before, the evergreens powdered with white. He remembered dragging his little sled out here, getting a huge running start as he glided down the lawn's slight incline. Not exactly a dare-devil ride. But then he wasn't much of a daredevil.

Yeah, no kidding.

He switched the engine off, scanned the snowy fields broken by fences, trees, low stone walls. A crow flew by, then another.

No point sitting there any longer. He got out of the car, bounded up the front steps, not glancing down at the place Hannah had fallen, not allowing himself to linger on the memories of her body in his arms, the snowflakes on her lashes...

His key went easily into the lock; he'd have to surrender his keys, too. When he drove away, the house would belong to someone else. Rita had contacted the movers who'd start carting off the furniture on Friday, putting it in storage until he felt settled and could decide what he wanted to keep and where.

For an odd confusing moment as he crossed the threshold, he felt he was letting his family down. Ha! The ultimate joke. What loyalty did he owe the Brattle name? Most of his life it hadn't even been his.

Inside, he glanced around, not wanting to dwell on the sights or the past.

"Hey, there." Smiling, Rita hurried to greet him wearing her usual black pants and bright sweater—yellow today. She wrapped her strong plump arms around his ribs, practically as high as she could reach. From the way she'd sounded when he'd spoken to her from Chicago, he expected her to look much more upset on this occasion. "It's wonderful to see you, Jack. How was the flight?"

"Adequate. It's good to see you, too, Rita. You look great. I thought you'd be in mourning."

"I am, but only halfway."

Ray approached from the hallway behind her, tall, bearded, beaming, extending a hand for a hearty shake. "Hello, Jack, welcome."

"Ray and I had our offer accepted on a beautiful house in Eugene, Oregon, this morning, so I'm both happy and not. We're all ready for a change, I guess."

Derek nodded, gripping Ray's hand, a thickening in his throat. "It's time."

"Are you sure, Jack?" Rita's cheery face dimmed with concern. "Really sure?"

"Rita…"

"Okay, okay." She lifted her hands in surrender. "Mrs. Jansen is here already, come on into the study."

He preceded her and Ray into the workroom his father and

grandfather and great-great-grandfather had also used as a cigar-puffery and general male retreat. Dark wood, leather chairs, a manly man's dream. He used to creep in and sit on the floor playing while his father worked, trying to be so quiet that Mr. Brattle Sr. wouldn't notice and kick him out, which he invariably did.

To the left of a thirty-something man in a badly fitting suit clutching a stack of documents, whom Jack assumed was Mrs. Jansen's lawyer, sat Mrs. Jansen herself. One look made his gut tighten. Much younger than he expected, barely thirty if that. Classic trophy wife, he'd bet she was her husband's second or third go-around with marriage—the older the guy got, the younger he married them. She had perfect faux-blond hair. Way too much makeup. Expensive clothing made to look casual. Brittle smile. Even his mother, appearance-obsessed during her good years, had a natural air of class and dignity. This woman was trying way too hard. Not what the house was about.

"Derek Gibson, this is Alice Jansen." Rita gestured to the next owner of the Brattle mansion who was watching him closely. He wouldn't give her the satisfaction of showing what he felt, though she must know. "I've explained that you have power of attorney for Jack Brattle in the sale."

"Yes. You have." The woman rose from the table and smiled the smile of a woman with self-confidence, forced charm and plans for as-needed plastic surgery in order to hang on to her marital meal ticket. "So nice to meet you, Mr. Gibson. I absolutely love your house. I can't wait to get my hands on it."

He forced himself to return her smile, uneasy over her choice of words. Rita and Ray had kept the house in meticulous repair. "Great."

"This room." She gestured around, eyes alight. "Is so wonderful. I absolutely love it."

Derek nodded, pleased. The room was one of his favorites, too. At least she appreciated what she was getting.

"It's going to be my yoga room. I'm going to simplify, simplify, simplify. Tear out all this heavy wood and shelving and paint in a calming sea-green with a hint of pistachio. Then I'm thinking Japanese-style minimalist furniture. Lots of bamboo and painted salvaged metal. Really organic."

Derek's smile froze. The idea of the century-old woodwork being turned into a New Age paean to self-indulgence made him sick.

"That lovely library next door we're going to turn into an entertainment center. We have a seventy-inch plasma TV, and my husband has a collection of over a thousand tapes and DVDs."

There were hundreds of volumes in there, Derek's favorites being those that were leather-bound with gilt lettering, yellowing hand-cut pages, several rare editions. He used to spend hours going through them. Books belonged there. "He doesn't read?"

"Who, Henry?" She let out a peal of laughter that grated on his nerves. "Never. Then the dining room I want to redo in bright red, the kitchen in yellow, the upstairs, oh my gosh, I'm *so* in my primary color phase right now. The whole place needs an update. That third floor, I'm going to transform into one huge space for my interpretive dance studio. I still haven't figured out where to put the pottery or the kiln. Oh, and we're not green thumbs, so we'll put a hot tub and sauna in where your greenhouse is. Or maybe a racquetball court. It's going to be so fabulous. We'll also expand the garage over the back garden to house my husband's collection of antique cars."

"Won't you sit down, Mr. Gibson?" Rita held out a chair to the right of the lawyer. He could see the blame in her eyes, making him feel like a pet owner bringing the vet a young healthy dog to put down because it no longer suited him. She needn't have bothered. The described renovations hit him hard, as well.

He sat, stared blankly at the huge pile of forms the lawyer shoved in front of him and proceeded to explain. He barely listened. A pottery studio? Meditation room? No more greenhouse?

"...if you'll just sign here, first, Mr. Gibson."

He took the offered pen, staring at the signature line. Every instinct in his body was screaming at him not to sign. To tell the tacky trophy wife to go home to her husband and pick on someone else's house. On someone else's *home.*

Was this good instinct or just his natural avoidance of change? His idiotic fear of letting go of his protection? Or a you-don't-know-what-you've-got-till-it's-gone warning he should pay attention to?

"What's the matter, Mr. Gibson?" Mrs. Jansen's voice held a distinct edge. "Having second thoughts?"

He adjusted his grip on the pen, determined to go forward with the sale.

And still couldn't sign.

Hannah in his bedroom, in his shower, in his kitchen, arching in ecstasy on the potting table.

"Derek, it's not too late." Rita put her hand on his shoulder. "You don't have to sell."

If he didn't sell, he'd be saddled with the house. He'd have to keep it up, deal with the memories...

And there it was. Exactly what he needed to do. Stop running away and tackle the house, his memories and his past head-on. Acknowledge who he was, Jack Brattle, and take the damn risk of being himself for once, and forever, whether Hannah's article ever came out or not.

Power rose in him, and optimism. He'd find Hannah, tell her Derek Gibson had an unfortunate accident but that Jack

Brattle had stepped in to take his place. That he had a big house with no one to fill it, with a fabulous place upstairs made for as many kids as she wanted. If she said no, he'd back off, then come at her again and again until she gave in. She loved him. They belonged together. She was worth risking everything for, no matter how many times it took.

He raised his head, looked Mrs. Jansen straight in the eye. "I can't sign this."

"No?" To his complete shock, she smiled, an open, friendly smile of delight, nothing like the toothy grimaces earlier. "Well, that's a relief."

Derek—no, *Jack*—stared at her. "A relief."

"I can't afford the bathroom in a place like this."

Her lawyer gathered up the contract pages, chuckling. "You can't afford a toilet seat in a place like this."

He looked from one to the other, without a clue. "What is going on?"

Rita burst out in a laugh she'd apparently been holding back for a while. "Look at his face. I haven't had so much fun in years. Jack, dear, you've been had."

"I've been…" He stared at her, feeling utterly stupid.

"Had, dear. 'Owned' as the kids say today. 'Punked.'"

A light dawned. "You set me up."

"Mm-hm." She looked happier than he'd seen her in months. Maybe years. "I had a feeling maybe you didn't want to sell as much as you said you did."

"Congratulations." Mrs. Jansen leaned over and offered her hand. "The house is yours. I'm Daphne Baldwin, this is my fiancé, Paul Kronwitz. We're paupers in real life."

"Daphne." Jack's voice came out hoarsely. "Hannah's friend?"

She sent a sidelong wink to her fiancé. "Hannah who? Never heard of her."

"Holy…" He put his hands to his temples. "Rita, what is happening here?"

She put her arm around him, squeezed hard. "Come have something to eat. Now that you're not selling, it turns out I have a house full of food."

This would all make sense someday. He would see the humor, retell the story to his friends, family, grandchildren. For right now he was still disoriented. He'd made the very tough and grand decision not to sell the house and it turned out he was never in danger of selling it anyway. "You knew I'd crack."

"Not for sure." She glanced at her husband who was grinning so hard his beard was sticking out. "Ray was really nervous."

"No, I wasn't." He got up from the chair and joined them, thumped Jack on the back. "Good job, Jack."

He shook his head. "*Et tu,* Ray?"

"I knew you couldn't sell the old girl. Got to keep a Brattle in the Brattle home."

Jack gestured to the papers on the desk. "Forgeries? Boilerplate?"

"A few forms from the Internet." The not-lawyer Paul fanned them out on the wooden table. "Mostly blanks."

Yup. Mostly blanks. He still couldn't quite take this all in. He was relieved and annoyed and happy and something else he couldn't quite get a handle on.

"Come eat. A celebration dinner is set up in here."

He let Rita pull him toward the dining room, still stunned, not only by the trick, but by his own inability to sell the house. "Rita, how did you come up with this scheme? It's not like you to be so sneaky."

"No, it isn't." She grinned at him. "Jack, dear. Your fun is only just beginning. I was all for convincing you not to sell, but the setup wasn't my idea."

"Then who—"

"Aren't you going to come in?" A familiar female voice spoke from his—*his*—dining room. "Food's getting cold."

He froze for two beats, then turned abruptly away from giggling Rita and walked through the doorway. Hannah stood next to the huge table his family had only used on major holidays or for the rare times they'd entertained, wearing jeans, a soft blue sweater that matched her eyes and a nervously welcoming smile. He'd never seen anything more beautiful in his life.

Why was she here? To see the fun? Watch him be on the receiving end of a revenge joke like the one he pulled on her? Or to ask those damn interview questions?

Or…

He couldn't ask in front of everyone. He'd have to play along for now.

"Hello, Derek."

He put his hands in his pockets and gazed at her. "It's Jack."

"Oh, it's *Jack* now?"

"Yes." He hid a cringe. "From now on, Hannah."

"What happened to Derek?"

"Ah, very sad. A fatal illness."

"Ooh." She winced. "Terrible."

"So that charade…" He pointed back over his shoulder. "That was your idea?"

"Rita called me." She smiled at Rita who'd come to stand beside him, that smile women share when they acknowledge between themselves what idiots men are. "She said you needed rescuing from yourself."

"Is that so?" He displayed his best tough-guy face to Rita who shrugged.

"You heard it here."

"So you lured me here under false pretenses." He turned back to Hannah, pretending outrage. "How could you?"

"Yeah, imagine that," she said wryly. "Can't think of *anyone* who would do something that low."

He ambled around to the other side of the table, wanting to touch her, wanting to talk to her in private, but doomed apparently to sharing a meal celebrating his purchase of his own house. "I hear you have more questions for me."

"Oh. Yes."

"For the interview?"

"Yes."

He dragged his eyes away from her, unable to gauge her mood or intentions, aware it was ridiculous to expect her to say, *Forget the interview, I just want you,* when there were four other people with carefully discreet eyes on the Hannah and Jack show.

Frowning, he stared at the meal until he registered what he was seeing and started to laugh.

Deviled eggs, pigs in blankets, tuna macaroni salad, chips, baked beans, all on colored plastic platters he'd never seen before. Bottles of orange soda and root beer. And a bakery cake that said Welcome Home in translucent green icing script on blindingly white frosting.

The most fabulous spread he'd ever seen. "Wow. This looks amazing."

"Rita helped me." Hannah came closer to the table and to him, which made him want to cart her off away from these people and this occasion and make love to her until time ended or he stopped wanting to, which could be a close call.

"Ha! I did nothing but supply our highest quality plastic." Rita waved her comment away. "Dig in, everyone."

"I'm starving." Daphne led Paul to the table. "Bad acting takes a lot out of me."

They ate around the table on paper plates with plastic utensils, laughing and talking. Jack joined in superficially, preoccupied with the situation involving Hannah. Judging by the numerous concerned glances shot in his and her direction from the other side of the table, he wasn't the only one. He tried to keep his own gaze on his food and on his friends, but the need to remind himself Hannah was really there, that she'd really materialized to help make sure he stayed in town—for whatever reason—made it nearly impossible not to stare, not to drink in the sight of her. When she spilled baked beans down her beautiful femininely curving front, it was all he could do not to offer his hands to clean her up.

Finally the last piece of achingly sweet cake had been eaten, the last drop of sugary soda swallowed. Rita and Ray cleaned up with lightning speed, refusing offers of help, then pointedly stayed in the kitchen. Daphne and Paul chatted briefly, made their excuses and left for some dubious appointment in an apparent hurry.

Obviously he and Hannah were supposed to talk alone. He couldn't be more grateful.

"Well."

"So." She smiled, this time with an undercurrent of anxiety. Was she afraid he'd want more or afraid he wouldn't?

He felt himself starting to shut down, to retreat into the protection of impassivity.

No. No. Not anymore.

"Come with me." He got up, took her hand. "Can you do stairs or do you need the elevator?"

"Stairs are fine if we go slowly. Where are we going?"

"You'll see." On the second floor he gestured her toward the continuation of the staircase. "One more."

"Upstairs? To your old room?"

"Yes."

"Why?"

"To play."

She stopped on the staircase. "To play."

"Yup." He gave in to his need to touch her, put his arm around her waist to make her climb easier. Yeah, that was it. Purely thinking of her comfort. "Bet I can beat you at Ping-Pong."

"Ha!" Her head snapped around; she glared at him, eyes shining. "No way. I was a Ping-Pong champion in my high school."

"You were?"

"No." She wrinkled her nose. "Sounded good, though, didn't it?"

"You had me seriously worried." He guided her through to the Ping-Pong room, feeling giddy, as if he'd had a bottle of champagne.

"Prepare to lose." He grabbed a ball and bounced it off the table a few times, then narrowed his eyes threateningly. "No, worse. Prepare to be humiliated."

As it happened, the humiliation was nearly his. Hannah played a mean game, and they were neck and neck to the end until he finally hit a shot she couldn't reach.

"Ha! Mine!"

"Oh, sure, you beat a cripple, congratulations." She put her paddle down, jammed her hands on her hips. "But there is no way you can beat me at pool."

She was right. He didn't have a chance. He also lost at checkers, gin rummy and even at Sorry! He'd never had this much fun, he was sure of it. At some point he'd have to get serious, but right now this time together was too perfect, too right. If nothing else, if she was still hesitating, this reminder of how good they were together couldn't hurt.

"Karaoke time." He strode from the game room toward the party music room.

"Oh, no." Hannah hung back, shaking her head. "You're not getting me to sing. No way."

"Oh, what, so I have to lose at games I'm bad at, but you don't?"

"You can't be *bad* at Sorry!" She limped into the room with him. "Just unlucky. Which also describes anyone who has heard me sing. You've never had that displeasure."

"No, I haven't." He turned on the machine, which sprang to life how many years after its last use? "But I'm about to."

"Derek—"

"Jack."

"Jack." She beamed at him. "Jack Brattle."

"Oh, by the way, that's me. Did I mention that?"

Her laughter lifted him impossibly higher. He knew without a doubt that if she gave them a chance, a hundred years with this woman wasn't going to be enough. "I think so. One of those Spider-Man-to-Mary Jane, Superman-to-Lois Lane confession scenes about the secret identity."

"Sing, Lois." He handed her the microphone.

"Jack, I am not going to—"

"Yes, you are. Here. I picked this just for you." He started the song "Wind Beneath My Wings," backed up and sat expectantly.

Hannah covered her mouth with her hand, the blush spreading up her cheeks. "Oh, man. This is going to be horrible."

"Go."

"Okay, okay. But remember, you asked for this." She started to sing. Or something close to it. Pitch was not her strength. Or tone. Or rhythm. But she stood there for him and sang because he wanted her to, and he didn't think he'd ever loved her as much as he did right then.

The final note she held, a quarter tone flat and wobbling, until the music ended, then put the microphone down in obvious relief. "No matter how long I know you, I am never ever doing that again, so don't even think about asking me."

"Yeah, um, I think you're safe there." He winked and stood to take her place.

She laughed again, face pink, and when she passed him on the way to the spectator seat, it was all he could do not to haul her into his arms and kiss her. But they had a few things to talk over first, and if he started kissing her now, he wasn't going to stop.

He selected a CD, skipped to the last song, "I've Got You Under My Skin," turned up the volume and, praying he didn't make a fool of himself, then suddenly not caring, he sang his heart out.

She giggled nervously at first, seeming unsure where to look. Yes, the moment was pretty sappy, but it was their moment. He walked toward her, holding her gaze, making her understand that this wasn't about the performance, that he meant every word. *So deep you're really a part of me.*

If she was just here for more interview questions, if she didn't want him, okay, but at least he hadn't hidden in safety. He was taking the risk, letting her know how he still felt, that his offer of sharing his life still held, for however long they lasted—and he'd bet on forever.

He reached her, knelt in front of her, laid the microphone on the floor, took her hands, sang the last line of the song, "…under…my…skin."

The music stopped. He waited, watching her. She wasn't laughing. That was good. She wasn't pushing him away. Also good. She looked unsettled, a bit uncertain. He didn't know if that was good or not. A tear appeared in the corner of one mesmerizing blue eye. She shook her head, closing her eyes, and it trailed down her beautiful flushed cheek.

"That was…incredible, Jack. I didn't know you could sing."

"Aw, c'mon." He brushed the tear away, rose and drew her to standing, bent to kiss her forehead, her cheeks. "It's just that after you anyone would sound like Pavarotti."

Hannah burst out laughing, face lit with delight, and his patience ran out. He cupped the back of her head and brought her mouth to his, kissed the laughter out of her until she was clinging to him, panting and sweet.

Then she wrapped her arms around his neck, pressed close and the sweetness was replaced by desire so hot he had to breathe deeply to keep from ravishing her.

"Jack." She tipped her head back to give him better access to her smooth throat. "Make love to me."

"You sure?"

"Oh, yes."

"You're not just here for the interview?"

"Are you serious?" She drew back and gave him an annoyed look. "You're not going to start that sex-for-interview stuff again."

"I want to hear it."

"I don't care if the interview never runs. I just want you."

He grinned, couldn't stop, took both of her hands into his and kissed them together. "That'll work."

"Did you miss the whole symbolism of the meal downstairs?"

"Lowbrow…" He looked to her for further explanation.

"And highbrow. Deviled eggs in a mansion. You and me. Together. See how it works?"

"Do I have to eat that kind of cake? Ever again? Because it was horrible."

She giggled and put her arms back around him where they belonged. "No, but you have to make love to me nearly every day."

"Oh. No." He spoke with flat exaggeration, rolling his eyes. "Anything but that."

"Jack…" She was looking at him seriously now. "Do you want me to run the interview?"

He already knew the answer. "Yes."

"Really?"

"Will you be here with me to share the fallout?"

"Try and get rid of me."

"Not on your life. And, yes, really." The decision was made, what's more, she'd let him make it. It was time for Jack Brattle's life to start. "Now that's settled. What were you saying earlier?"

"About the interview?" She blinked innocently.

"Nope. Before that."

"The cake?"

"Hmm, no. Not that, either." He lifted her sweater, ran his hands up and down her smooth firm skin. "Before."

"Oh, wow, I'm not sure I remember…" She moved seductively against his fly. "Maybe it will come to me."

"Maybe it will come in you."

"Yes, please," she whispered. "Yes, please, Jack."

He undressed her reverently, kissing the skin he uncovered, kneeling to taste where he couldn't resist tasting, so full of emotion at being able to be with her like this that he felt more humble than when she'd beaten him at pretty much everything.

And when she was beautifully and totally naked, he picked her up and carried her to his childhood bed, where he'd spent many adolescent nights dreaming of exactly this scenario— only completely without a clue as to details.

"I missed you." He laid her on the navy-and-white geometric quilt, smiled down at her, taking off his jacket.

"I missed you, too."

"Hmm." He got rid of his shoes, socks, pants. "Disappearing is a strange way of showing it."

"I know." She stroked his thighs, trailed gentle fingers around his hips while he took off his shirt, her face troubled. "At first I felt I was being stronger by leaving you. I was sick and tired of feeling weak with men. Then I realized it wasn't a question of strength, it was a question of getting out of the rut of my own perception and welcoming yours in. Did you read my Lowbrow column?"

"Of course." He shed the rest of his clothes and joined her on the bed, hardly daring to believe he could hold her again.

"Did you get the message?"

"I thought so. When you didn't answer my call, and didn't leave me any way to reach you, I thought…well, I didn't know what to think."

"I wanted to tell you in the column first. And then, um, Rita called me, and by that time…"

He shook his head. "Scheming wench. You knew you'd get me tonight."

"I certainly hoped I'd get you, yes." She pulled his head down for a kiss. He fitted himself to her body, his erection, in its usual base way, desperate to cut to the chase.

"I have a condom in the night table." He whispered into her hair, kissing the strands, inhaling the sweet citrus-Hannah scent.

"Oh, good."

"From the eighties."

She cracked up. "Oh, bad."

"I have a suggestion." He raised up and gazed at her tenderly, drew his hand down between her breasts, lingering over her stomach. "I've used condoms consistently with other women."

She drew in a slow breath, met his eyes and nodded. "I tested clean after my last boyfriend cheated. And I can't get pregnant right now."

"I want this relationship to last a lifetime, Hannah." He took her hand, watching carefully for her reaction.

"I want that, too." Her eyes filled up, but he didn't feel the need to comfort her for those tears.

"Hannah, will you…" he kissed the tip of one finger and gave her an overly sappy stare "…not use a condom with me?"

Her giggles stopped the tears. "I do."

She did. He kissed her, then forgot to stop kissing her, or maybe he was unable to. He touched her everywhere, wanting to own her, to make sure she knew her body belonged to him and only him. Until she wriggled down and her lips surrounded his penis. She sucked in the length of him, then back, then in again, and his caveman impulses were reduced to nothing.

Never mind. He was hers. Completely and helplessly hers, giving in to the pleasure of her mouth on him until he sensed his climax approaching too soon.

"Up here, with me." He took her gently by the shoulders and shifted her back up next to him. "Are you ready?"

"Oh, yes." She spread her legs, naked to him. He moved over her, his erection naked to her, and his heart swelled. They were committing to each other, in a way modern times made significant. He didn't think he could be happier.

Except when he slid slowly inside her, skin to skin, and he realized he could be.

"I love you." The words came out of him before he'd planned to say them. "It's improbable, impossible, insane, but I fell in love with you first through your words. Meeting you only made it official."

"I fell in love with you at first sight, too, Jack." She took a shuddering breath, hugged him to her, buried her face in his neck. "Then, of course, I had to fall in love with Derek, and then with you *again,* but I managed."

"Wow." He smiled and kissed her temple. "So we're actually having a threesome?"

"No." She moaned as he began to move faster. "It's just you and me, Jack Brattle."

"Well, Ms. Hannah O'Reilly." He slid his hands under her perfect ass and made her moan again. "It's pretty risky to commit like this when we don't know each other well. Only twenty-four hours together."

"I know." She opened her eyes, looked deeply into his as he moved inside her. "It's crazy, spontaneous, wild."

"Any doubts?"

"About diving right in?" She smiled and wrapped her legs around his back. "Not a single one."

Epilogue

Transcript of the *Laina Live* show, October 24, Channel 25

Laina: Hello, and welcome to *Laina Live!* I have two very special guests today whose names you know, though you might not know their faces quite as well, since most of the public has only met them on the written page. Mr. Jack Brattle and Ms. Hannah O'Reilly. Welcome to the show!

Jack: Hi, Laina.

Hannah: We're glad to be here.

Laina: So these two have a *stupendously* fascinating past and a totally made-for-movie romance. Unless you lived under a rock for the past year, you already know it. He tricked her into showing up at his house, the frog turned out to be a prince, and they're on their way to happy ever after. Let me start off with you, Hannah. You wrote the article that introduced Jack Brattle to the world. That was *such* a big deal, it seems like every paper in the universe ran it. Now rumor has it you're on the shortlist for the *Pulitzer!* How does that feel?

Hannah: Like there has to be some mistake? No, actually it's amazing. I'm thrilled and terrified.

Laina: I have to tell this audience that if you haven't read the article, *go find it* online. It's so, so much more than a celebrity tell-all. Hannah tackles money issues, social responsibility issues, class issues, materialism, the importance of living life to its fullest, she even takes America to task over its obsession with celebrity. Just a really, really deep article. Go read it. *Go! Now!*

Hannah: Thank you.

Laina: Jack, did you expect the article to be that far-reaching?

Jack: I knew Hannah would write a good article. I watched her slave over it. So I expected to be impressed, but even so, I was blown away. It meant a lot to me.

Laina: I'll say. It meant you were suddenly in the public eye where we hadn't seen a Brattle since your father, right?

Jack: Yes, he enjoyed the attention.

Laina: And you didn't. So how has the fallout been for you?

Jack: At times overwhelming. I thought I was prepared, but you can't really understand what it's like to live under a microscope until you have to do it. I have no idea why anyone would want to do a reality TV show.

Laina: Not lining up for that any time soon, huh?

Jack: Uh, no. I'm living it now, and it's plenty.

Laina: Jack, I know you hid yourself away for a lot of years especially after your father's death. Do you regret that now? Or do you wish you were still in hiding?

Jack: There are moments I wish I could go back to being anonymous. But it was time to own up to who I am and take the responsibilities that came with that. Hiding was safer, but I was living someone else's life. I don't regret the decision to own up to my name. And Hannah has been there for me, so I'm not going it alone.

Laina: Yeah, so what's it been like for you, Hannah, to be a total and complete *star* by association?

Hannah: There are days I really feel for all those celebrities who've ever punched out a paparazzo. But most days I take a deep breath and remind myself that in the big picture, this is what we want, and they can't possibly want to film us walking down the street to buy tissues and dog food forever.

Laina: Now it's everyone's absolute *favorite* part of your story that you two are involved with each other, after the dueling columns in the newspapers, et cetera, et cetera. How do you think your relationship affected the Jack Brattle article, Hannah?

Hannah: I was definitely able to get to know Jack better than if I were just his interviewer. I don't recommend every reporter try to get that close to her subject, but in this case it brought me a truly intimate understanding of what his life had been like as a kid, how that upbringing and his parents' tragedies affected him, then and now, and the struggles he was fighting for so many years. I got to see all that in his decisions and choices as they related to me. I admire him a lot for deciding to take the step of going public.

Laina: Sounds like he's an inspiration.

Hannah: Oh, definitely. At the risk of sounding like a bride-to-be cliché, he's the most amazing man I've ever met.

Laina: Aww. Say it with me, audience. *Aww.* And, Jack, she's inspired you, too, can you tell us how?

Jack: She inspired me to stop hiding from my life.

Laina: Oh, that deserves another very sincere "Aww." Can we get it audience? *Aww.* Good job, thank you. Now, Hannah, *what* is your next article on?

Hannah: I'm investigating some promising medications that should be available to the general public—but aren't.

Laina: I'm not allowed to ask more, am I?

Hannah: No, sorry!

Laina: And, of course, what we all want to know is about your wedding plans.

Jack: We're getting married next June. And that's all I'm going to—

Hannah: The Philadelphia Cathedral on June 8. Everyone's invited.

Jack: *Hannah.*

Hannah: What, you can't afford it?

Jack: (Unintelligible mutter.) The reception is private anyway.

Hannah: Yes. Caviar and onion soup-mix dip for a hundred.

Jack: Filet mignon and hot dogs.

Hannah: Chili dogs, mmm.

Laina: It is to die for! Well, Hannah and Jack, I have a million more questions, but we're out of time. We wish you many, many years of happiness together. It's wonderful to have the Brattles as an active part of Philadelphia again.

Jack: Thank you, Laina.

Hannah: Thanks for having us.

Laina: This is *Laina Live*, you all come back after this commercial break 'cuz *I will still be here!*

* * * * *

*Celebrate 60 years of pure reading pleasure
with Harlequin® Books!*

*Harlequin Romance® is celebrating by showering you with
DIAMOND BRIDES in February 2009.
Six stories that promise to bring a touch of sparkle to your
life, with diamond proposals and dazzling weddings,
sparkling brides and gorgeous grooms!*

*Enjoy a sneak peek at Caroline Anderson's
TWO LITTLE MIRACLES,
available February 2009 from Harlequin Romance®.*

'I'VE FOUND HER.'

Max froze.

It was what he'd been waiting for since June, but now—now he was almost afraid to voice the question. His heart stalling, he leaned slowly back in his chair and scoured the investigator's face for clues. 'Where?' he asked, and his voice sounded rough and unused, like a rusty hinge.

'In Suffolk. She's living in a cottage.'

Living. His heart crashed back to life, and he sucked in a long, slow breath. All these months he'd feared—

'Is she well?'

'Yes, she's well.'

He had to force himself to ask the next question. 'Alone?'

The man paused. 'No. The cottage belongs to a man called John Blake. He's working away at the moment, but he comes and goes.'

God. He felt sick. So sick he hardly registered the next few words, but then gradually they sank in. 'She's got *what?*'

'Babies. Twin girls. They're eight months old.'

'Eight—?' he echoed under his breath. 'They must be his.'

He was thinking out loud, but the P.I. heard and corrected him.

'Apparently not. I gather they're hers. She's been there since mid-January last year, and they were born during the summer—June, the woman in the post office thought. She was more than helpful. I think there's been a certain amount of speculation about their relationship.'

He'd just bet there had. God, he was going to kill her. Or Blake. Maybe both of them.

'Of course, looking at the dates, she was presumably pregnant when she left you, so they could be yours, or she could have been having an affair with this Blake character before…'

He glared at the unfortunate P.I. 'Just stick to your job. I can do the math,' he snapped, swallowing the unpalatable possibility that she'd been unfaithful to him before she'd left. 'Where is she? I want the address.'

'It's all in here,' the man said, sliding a large envelope across the desk to him. 'With my invoice.'

'I'll get it seen to. Thank you.'

'If there's anything else you need, Mr Gallagher, any further information—'

'I'll be in touch.'

'The woman in the post office told me Blake was away at the moment, if that helps,' he added quietly, and opened the door.

Max stared down at the envelope, hardly daring to open it, but when the door clicked softly shut behind the P.I., he eased up the flap, tipped it and felt his breath jam in his throat as the photos spilled out over the desk.

Oh, lord, she looked gorgeous. Different, though. It took him a moment to recognise her, because she'd grown her hair, and it was tied back in a ponytail, making her look younger and somehow freer. The blond highlights were gone, and it was back to its natural soft golden-brown, with a little curl in the end of the ponytail that he wanted to thread his finger through and tug, just gently, to draw her back to him.

Crazy. She'd put on a little weight, but it suited her. She

looked well and happy and beautiful, but oddly, considering how desperate he'd been for news of her for the past year— one year, three weeks and two days, to be exact—it wasn't only Julia who held his attention after the initial shock. It was the babies sitting side by side in a supermarket trolley. Two identical and absolutely beautiful little girls.

* * * * *

When Max Gallagher hires a P.I. to find his estranged wife, Julia, he discovers she's not alone—she has twin baby girls, and they might be his. Now workaholic Max has just two weeks to prove that he can be a wonderful husband and father to the family he wants to treasure.

Look for TWO LITTLE MIRACLES by Caroline Anderson, available February 2009 from Harlequin Romance®.

CELEBRATE
60 YEARS
OF PURE READING PLEASURE
WITH HARLEQUIN®!

We'll be spotlighting a different series
every month throughout 2009
to celebrate our 60th anniversary.

Look for Harlequin® Romance in February!

**Harlequin® Romance is celebrating by showering
you with Diamond Brides in February 2009.**

Six stories that promise to bring a touch of sparkle to
your life, with diamond proposals and dazzling weddings,
sparkling brides and gorgeous grooms!

Collect all six books in February 2009,
featuring *Two Little Miracles* by Caroline Anderson.

*Look for the Diamond Brides miniseries
in February 2009!*

www.eHarlequin.com   HRBRIDES09

HARLEQUIN Romance®

This February the Harlequin® Romance series
will feature six Diamond Brides stories featuring
diamond proposals and gorgeous grooms.

Share your dream wedding proposal and you could WIN!

The most romantic entry will win a diamond
necklace and will inspire a proposal in one of
our upcoming Diamond Grooms books in 2010.

In 100 words or less, tell us the most romantic
way that you dream of being proposed to.

For more information, and to enter
the Diamond Brides Proposal contest, please visit
www.DiamondBridesProposal.com

Or mail your entry to us at:

IN THE U.S.: 3010 Walden Ave., P.O. Box 9069, Buffalo, NY 14269-9069
IN CANADA: 225 Duncan Mill Road, Don Mills, ON M3B 3K9

REQUEST YOUR FREE BOOKS!

2 FREE NOVELS
PLUS 2
FREE GIFTS!

HARLEQUIN®

Blaze™

Red-hot reads!

YES! Please send me 2 FREE Harlequin® Blaze™ novels and my 2 FREE gifts (gifts are worth about $10). After receiving them, if I don't wish to receive any more books, I can return the shipping statement marked "cancel." If I don't cancel, I will receive 6 brand-new novels every month and be billed just $4.24 per book in the U.S. or $4.71 per book in Canada; plus 25¢ shipping and handling per book and applicable taxes, if any*. That's a savings of 15% or more off the cover price! I understand that accepting the 2 free books and gifts places me under no obligation to buy anything. I can always return a shipment and cancel at any time. Even if I never buy another book, the two free books and gifts are mine to keep forever.

151 HDN ERVA 351 HDN ERUX

Name	(PLEASE PRINT)
Address	Apt. #
City	State/Prov.	Zip/Postal Code

Signature (if under 18, a parent or guardian must sign)

Mail to the **Harlequin Reader Service:**
IN U.S.A.: P.O. Box 1867, Buffalo, NY 14240-1867
IN CANADA: P.O. Box 609, Fort Erie, Ontario L2A 5X3

Not valid to current subscribers of Harlequin Blaze books.

Want to try two free books from another line?
Call 1-800-873-8635 or visit www.morefreebooks.com.

* Terms and prices subject to change without notice. N.Y. residents add applicable sales tax. Canadian residents will be charged applicable provincial taxes and GST. Offer not valid in Quebec. This offer is limited to one order per household. All orders subject to approval. Credit or debit balances in a customer's account(s) may be offset by any other outstanding balance owed by or to the customer. Please allow 4 to 6 weeks for delivery. Offer available while quantities last.

Your Privacy: Harlequin Books is committed to protecting your privacy. Our Privacy Policy is available online at www.eHarlequin.com or upon request from the Reader Service. From time to time we make our lists of customers available to reputable third parties who may have a product or service of interest to you. If you would prefer we not share your name and address, please check here. ☐

HB08R

COMING NEXT MONTH

#447 BLAZING BEDTIME STORIES Kimberly Raye, Leslie Kelly, Rhonda Nelson

Who said fairy tales are just for kids? Three intrepid Blaze heroines decide to take a break from reality—and discover, to their personal satisfaction, just how sexy happily-ever-afters can be....

#448 SOMETHING WICKED Julie Leto

Josie Vargas has always believed in love at first sight—and once she meets lawman Rick Fernandez, she's a goner. If only he didn't have those demons stalking him....

#449 THE CONCUBINE Jade Lee
Blaze Historicals

Chen Ji Yue has the chance to bring the ultimate honor to her family if she is chosen as one of the new emperor's wives. Of course, first she has to beat out the other three hundred virgins vying for the position. And then she has to stay out of the bed of Sun Bo Tao, the emperor's best friend.

#450 SHE THINKS HER EX IS SEXY... Joanne Rock
24 Hours: Lost

After a very public quarrel with her boyfriend, rock star Romeo Jinks, actress Shannon Leigh just wants to get her life back. But when she finds herself stranded in the Sonoran Desert with her ex, she learns that great sex can make breaking up hard to do.

#451 ABLE-BODIED Karen Foley
Uniformly Hot!

Delta Force operator Ransom Bennett is used to handling anything that comes his way. But debilitating headaches have put him almost out of action. Luckily, his new neighbor, Hannah Hartwell, knows how to handle his pain...and him, too.

#452 UNDER THE INFLUENCE Nancy Warren
Forbidden Fantasies

Sexy bartender Johnny Santini mixes one wicked martini. Or so business exec Natalie Fanshaw discovers, sitting at his bar one lonely Valentine's night. Could a fling with him be a recipe for disaster? Well, she could always claim to be under the influence....

HBCNMBPA0109R2